Eli stepped out of his vehicle and tied up his horse.

She blushed. The two-wheeled carriage he'd driven resembled the type used for courting. He grinned when he saw her standing a few yards away.

"Martha! *Guder mariye!*" He looked glad to see her.

"*Gut* morning, Eli. Working alone today?"

"*Ja.* Isaac is helping *Dat* on the farm."

"Why aren't you helping your *vadder*?"

"He says he doesn't need my help. I'd rather be here. You pay me to work." His smile held pure masculine appreciation.

Was Eli flirting with her?

"What are you planning to do today?" she asked as he continued to smile at her.

"Finish a few items on *Dat*'s list." He studied her for a long moment. His smile disappeared. "I'll get to work."

As she pinned up some towels on the clothesline, she flashed a look in Eli's direction. *What is it about this man that makes me unable to ignore him?* She recalled the two men in her life who had hurt her.

Not again. It wouldn't happen a third time. Not with anyone.

Rebecca Kertz was first introduced to the Amish when her husband took a job with an Amish construction crew. She enjoyed watching the Amish foreman's children at play and swapping recipes with his wife. Rebecca resides in Delaware with her husband and dog. She has a strong faith in God and feels blessed to have family nearby. Besides writing, she enjoys reading, doing crafts and visiting Lancaster County.

Books by Rebecca Kertz

Love Inspired

Lancaster County Weddings

Noah's Sweetheart
Jedidiah's Bride
A Wife for Jacob
Elijah and the Widow

Lancaster Courtships

The Amish Mother

Elijah and
the Widow

Rebecca Kertz

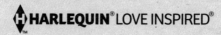

Recycling programs
for this product may
not exist in your area.

 LOVE INSPIRED BOOKS

ISBN-13: 978-0-373-81900-3

Elijah and the Widow

Copyright © 2016 by Rebecca Kertz

This edition published by arrangement with Love Inspired Books.

® and TM are trademarks of Love Inspired Books, used under license.
Trademarks indicated with ® are registered in the United States Patent
and Trademark Office, the Canadian Intellectual Property Office and in
other countries.

www.Harlequin.com

Printed in U.S.A.

Complete my joy by being of the same mind,
having the same love, being in full accord
and of one mind.
—*Philippians* 2:2

For Melissa Endlich, Editor Extraordinaire, for her kind patience, understanding and expertise. Thank you.

Chapter One

Happiness, Lancaster County,
Pennsylvania
Spring

The winter had been fierce with heavy snowstorms and time spent huddled near the woodstoves in the gathering room and in the kitchen. Elijah Lapp was glad to see the bitter cold weather end. He stood on the edge of the family farm, lifted his face toward the sun and closed his eyes. He inhaled deeply and smiled. The warm breeze felt good against his skin, and he enjoyed the scents of spring blossoms and freshly tilled dirt, a clear reminder of nature's rebirth.

The sound of distant male voices had him opening his eyes. *Dat* and his younger brothers headed in his direction. His father handled the reins to the four big chestnut Belgians that pulled the plow while Isaac walked alongside the horses, ready to help maneuver them as they reached the end of the field. Daniel and Joseph, the youngest, trailed behind. He heard laughter as Daniel jostled Joseph teasingly. *Dat* scolded the two boys, and they grinned at each other as they returned to work.

Eli chuckled and shook his head. He remembered when Jacob and he were learning farmwork. They had walked with *Dat* and listened as their father had explained how to get the most from the soil. He smiled as he recalled how excited he'd been when *Dat* had given him the leathers for the first time. To be allowed to operate the farm equipment had made him feel like a man.

He watched as *Dat* steered the plow to the end of a field before Isaac grabbed hold of the gear to lead the horses in the opposite direction. He should be working with them today, but Noah had asked for assistance with his furniture business, and *Dat* said Eli could go because he had enough help for the day's planned work.

His father acknowledged him with a nod when he saw him. Eli waved as Samuel Lapp slowed the horses to within a few yards of where he stood. The large draft horses halted on command, and *Dat* turned to him with a smile.

"*Dat*, I'll be leaving now. Are you sure you don't need me to stay?"

Samuel took off his straw hat and wiped his brow with his shirtsleeve. "*Ja*, but I'll need your help tomorrow."

"I wouldn't go today, but Noah is eager to catch up with his work orders."

His father settled his hat back onto his head. "You're becoming skilled as a cabinetmaker in your own right," he said, sounding pleased.

Eli smiled. He enjoyed working with his hands, and he was thankful that his brother had given him the opportunity to craft a few wooden chairs and a number of tables. "The only things I'll be making for him today are deliveries."

Noah and his wife, Rachel, had recently welcomed a baby girl—Katherine, named after his mother, the baby's grandmother. Little Katy was the joy of her parents' lives. Since her miscarriage two years ago, his sister-in-law had feared that she'd never be able to carry a child to full term. But everything had gone smoothly with Katy's birth. A proud father, his brother Noah hoped to finish his deliveries early so that he could spend time with Rachel and their infant daughter.

"Ever think of joining Noah as a cabinetmaker?" *Dat* asked.

"*Nay.* I want a business of my own." Eli had

been saving most of what he'd been allowed to keep from his earnings since he was eleven. Soon he'd have enough money to finance his own carriage shop. He'd known what he wanted to do ever since he'd been given an old courting buggy that shopkeeper Bob Whittier discovered in an outbuilding on his new property. Eli took work wherever he could, whether it was helping in the furniture shop or working on a construction crew for the company who occasionally employed his eldest brother, Jedidiah.

"I want to make and fix buggies and wagons." Lapp's Buggy Shop was his dream, and Eli wasn't about to give it up.

"Opening a business is not easy, *soohn*. You should consider working with Noah," *Dat* said. "Now that he has a family, your *bruder* may want to take on a partner. There will come a day when you will want to settle down."

"Someday," Eli said. But not now. There was no one special in his life. While he enjoyed the company of several girls at singings and church gatherings, he hadn't found the one he wanted to spend the rest of his life with. And until he had a successful business, which he hoped would be sooner rather than later, he wasn't going to get serious with any girl. "I should go. Noah will be wondering why I'm late, and Jacob asked me to stop by on my way." He started toward the barnyard, then halted and turned when his father spoke.

"Think about what I said." Samuel rubbed his whiskered chin.

"I will." He would think about partnering with Noah because his father had asked him to, but he doubted he'd change his mind. "I'll see you later, *Dat*."

With a nod, his father returned to his plow, and Eli climbed into the family's open market wagon and headed toward his brother's house, a small cottage on the edge of Horseshoe Joe's property. He slowed his vehicle as he approached Jacob's driveway. He wondered why his twin had asked him to come. Joe Zook, Jacob's mentor, had invited Jacob into his blacksmith business two years ago after Jacob had stepped in to run Zook's Blacksmithy while Joe recuperated from a serious leg injury. Since then he'd married the woman he'd always loved, Joe's daughter Annie. His brother was blessed, and Eli was happy for him.

Jacob exited the house as Eli parked the buggy close to his brother's cottage. "Jacob! *Hallo!*" He climbed out of his vehicle.

"Right on time." His brother smiled as he approached. "I appreciate you stopping. Annie wants to visit Martha King with EJ. I have to work at the shop. I don't want her out and about alone. I thought you could bring her since you're headed that way."

Martha's farm was located between their house and Noah's home and business. "I'd be happy to take her." He understood Jacob's concern. In the last trimester of her pregnancy, Annie was carrying their second child. EJ, Eli's namesake and Jacob and Annie's firstborn, was a toddler, and Eli realized that his brother didn't want his pregnant wife driving their buggy while trying to manage their extremely active twelve-month-old son. "Do you need me to bring her home?"

"*Nay.* She'll only be there a few hours. I should be able to slip away after I finish up with Amos's mare and William Mast's gelding. If I can't get away, I'll send Peter to bring her home."

Annie came out of the house, holding her young son's hand. "Eli! I'm surprised to see you here. Anything wrong?"

"*Nay.*" Jacob spoke up before Eli could answer. "Eli came to drive you to Martha's."

She scowled at her husband, but her loving look said that his concern pleased her. "Jacob, you worry too much."

Jacob regarded her with warmth. "You're my wife. I'll always be concerned about you."

She heaved a sigh. "If you insist, I'll go with your *bruder.*" She addressed Eli. "Would you mind holding your nephew while I fetch a plate of brownies?"

"With pleasure." Eli beamed as he lifted the little boy into his arms. "*Hallo* there, Elijah John." He bounced the child until EJ gurgled with laughter. He recalled how pleased he'd been when Annie and Jacob had chosen to name their firstborn son after him. The fact that EJ had his coloring, blond hair and blue eyes, gave him cause to frequently tease his brother and sister-in-law. While he and Jacob were twin brothers, they looked nothing alike. They were fraternal twins. Jacob's hair was as dark as his was golden. His brother had brown eyes while his were blue. Of course, EJ's coloring might have been inherited from his fair-haired, blue-eyed mother and not his uncle. But it wouldn't be any fun if he couldn't tease his brother. "He's growing so fast."

"*Ja*, soon he'll be as big as you," Jacob joked, and Eli laughed.

Annie returned seconds later with the wrapped brownies. Jacob took the plate from her and set it in the back of the vehicle. He helped her up onto the bench seat of the wagon while Eli carried EJ around to the other side. He set his nephew in the middle of the seat beside Annie. He then slid in next to the boy and picked up the leathers.

"Be careful," Jacob warned.

Annie shot him an irritated look. "He's only driving us down the road, Jacob. I could have walked."

Eli looked at her. "With EJ?" It would have been too far for her to walk with EJ.

Jacob eyed his wife with patience. "I want you to be safe," he said, his expression tender.

"I know you do." Annie blinked rapidly as if fighting tears. "You will come for me later?"

"Ja." Jacob leaned closer to her through the open window. "If I can't get away, I'll send Peter," he told her, referring to Annie's younger sibling. He eyed Eli from across the vehicle. *"Danki, bruder."*

"You're *willkomm*, Jacob." Eli waited as Jacob straightened before he flicked the leathers and drove off. Annie was quiet beside him as they left, but his nephew babbled incessantly in what sounded like baby Pennsylvania *Deitsch*, the language spoken within the Amish household. He shot them a glance as he steered his family's mare toward the King farm. As if sensing his attention, his sister-in-law turned from the window and met his gaze. She smiled, and he grinned back, his right hand reaching out to lightly ruffle EJ's hair while he returned his gaze to the increasingly busy road.

* * *

Martha Schrock King had opened the house windows to allow the warm spring breeze to filter in and freshen up the stale indoor air. She stood at her bedroom window, enjoying the light gust that caressed her face and rustled her clothing as she studied the yard below.

Spring had made her mark. The lawn was lush and green; the leaves on the trees were beginning to sprout light green while others showed the promise of rebirth in the tiny reddish-brown buds at the end of each tree branch.

She'd been alone in the house these past few weeks, and she was managing. There were memories of her husband in every room. She could almost hear his voice calling to her as he entered the house from outside. She and Ike had been married more than a year when he'd suffered a fatal heart attack while shoveling snow during an early heavy November snowstorm. During the winter months that followed, she'd had to come to grips with living the rest of her life alone. She would never know the joy of growing old with her husband nor experience the wonder of holding their baby son or daughter. But Ike's death was *Gottes wille* and she prayed to the Lord daily for the strength to accept it.

Martha shifted her attention toward her farm

fields. It was the season when families gathered to work up the soil and plant seed. Soon she'd have to find someone to help with the planting. She could appeal to the community, but the farm was hers, and eventually she would have to find a way to manage on her own. If she didn't, she might have to sell the property and go home to Indiana.

Thoughts of Indiana made her think briefly of her former betrothed, John Miller. She had cared for him deeply and she'd thought he'd felt the same. But then John had chosen to leave the Amish way of life—and her. She had joined the church and would have been shunned if she'd gone with him. *Not that he'd ever asked me.* The knowledge still made her feel a little pang whenever she recalled the day he'd told her that he was leaving.

Martha straightened her spine. She must accept that her life hadn't gone the way she'd envisioned. She had loved and lost two men—John and her husband, Ike. She sighed. There was no use questioning God's plan. She would find the strength to rise above the challenge to become self-sufficient. Fortunately, Ike had left her enough money to last for several months, perhaps even a year if she was careful. But she needed to discover a way to earn income before there was nothing left to buy supplies, care for the animals and maintain the house.

As she turned from the window, she caught a flicker of movement out of the corner of her eye. She groaned as she saw her first challenge. Two sheep had escaped from the pasture and were munching contently on the side lawn. Then she watched as her best dairy cow widened the fence opening as it followed the sheep.

Martha hurried downstairs. If she didn't put them back where they belonged, the animals might wander into the road. As she raced outside, she made a quick decision to corral the sheep first. She eased toward the closest one, and when the animal bolted out of reach, she ran after it. Her attempts to corner her livestock became an unwelcome game of cat and mouse between her and the sheep as she raced about the yard in hot pursuit.

The animal stopped several feet away. Martha paused to catch her breath, hoping that if she remained still for a few minutes, the sheep would become too busy eating to notice when she approached. She bent over and rested her hands on her knees, peering at them in watchful anticipation. Straightening slowly, she took a small step toward it and then stopped. When the animal didn't move, Martha eased closer, then froze when the sheep suddenly looked up from his food, gave her an evil look and took off. She spun toward the other lamb that stood within range, but it baaed loudly at her and scuttled away.

Determined, she gave chase, zigzagging back and forth in an attempt to block one and then the other's escape. The sheep ran toward her Holstein, and Martha shrieked in frustration as the cow mooed and shifted into a loping run. She found herself running after three animals instead of two. She became dismayed when she heard bleating and noted the escape of a fourth animal—Millicent, her temperamental milk goat.

"Move!" she hollered as she ran about waving her hands in an attempt to herd them in the right direction. "*Nay! Nay!* This way!"

"Shoo! Shoo!" a deep voice exclaimed, startling her.

Martha spun and saw Elijah Lapp, her friend Annie's brother-in-law, as he joined in the chase for her livestock. She gasped as something soft brushed past her—one of the escaped lambs.

Flashing her a grin, Eli raced after the animal. She started to follow but slowed when she spotted his vehicle parked in the dirt drive close to the farmhouse. Recognizing Annie seated in the market wagon with her young son, Martha waved at her before she renewed her efforts to capture and pen up her animals.

It felt like a comedy of errors to Martha as she and Eli ran about the yard in hot pursuit of four pesky farm critters. Eli reached to snatch the smaller lamb and nearly fell when it eluded his grasp. He righted himself as the lamb headed in her direction, and Martha extended her arms to capture it. She slipped to her knees but managed to get a firm grip on the sheep.

"Got him!" she cried. Triumphant, she grinned at Eli, who gave her a nod of approval before he went after the second lamb.

Where could she put it until the fence was repaired? Martha gave it some thought. *In the barn.* She fought to pick up the struggling animal as she stood, then stumbled into the building and locked it inside a stall before she left to rejoin Eli. Outside Eli had control of the cow and was urging her toward the barn.

"In the stable next to the sheep!" she instructed, and he immediately obeyed.

While Eli was inside the barn, Martha went after her wily goat. The beast bleated loudly as if daring Martha to capture her. Martha sprang forward just as the goat rammed into her. Taken by surprise, Martha wobbled and then fell face forward. She got a mouthful of grass and dirt as the animal took off behind her.

Martha rolled onto her side and lay a moment with her eyes closed. She counted to ten silently, unhappy to be bested by a stubborn she-goat. She thought she heard Annie cry out something, but she couldn't be sure.

Sensing someone above her, she looked up and saw Eli gazing down at her with concern. "Are you all right?" he said huskily. He crouched down to examine her more closely, and she felt the sharp impact of his bright azure eyes.

"*Ja*, I'm unhurt." She gave him a crooked smile. The only thing that ailed her was embarrassment.

Looking relieved, Eli rose and extended his hand toward her. Martha stared at it a moment, debating whether or not to accept his help. She lifted her gaze and noted his tousled hair along with the dirt streaks and grass clippings on his handsome face and on his clothing. Two animals were in their pens, but there were still two critters running loose. The young man's appearance and her own state of disarray with messy hair and grass-stained frock suddenly struck her as hilarious. She began to laugh. Her laughter started as a wide smile, then became a chuckle before it blossomed into a full-out belly-clutching roar.

She could sense that Eli was startled as he stared at her in silence with his hand still extended. Then his features crinkled with amusement, and his blue eyes began to twinkle. His chuckle turned into a laugh as if he, like her, had realized suddenly the hilarity in their situation—two grown adults bested by livestock.

Her laughter felt wonderful; it had been a while since she'd felt this good. Martha reached for his hand, and Eli pulled her to her feet. Her loud outburst eased to a soft giggle. Then the thought came to her that this wasn't proper behavior for a widow, and she quickly pulled herself together.

"What do *ya* think?" she asked him. "Can we get the last of them?"

"Ja." He grinned. "Can't let a couple of critters get the better of us."

Martha couldn't contain her chuckle. "I think they already have."

"Not for long!" he exclaimed as he spun and gave chase to the goat that dared to come too close. "Bet I can grab him first!"

"Not if I get to her before you do!" she cried, taking off after him. The goat continued to elude them. This was the most fun that Martha had enjoyed in years, and she wasn't going to feel guilty about it. She forgot about her sorrow and felt alive again, almost as if God was reminding her that she had her life to live.

Chapter Two

It took him and Martha over twenty minutes to capture the last two animals. While they chased them, Eli saw that his sister-in-law had climbed out of the buggy to wait. While he and Martha ran around, Annie kept her excited son firmly against her side while holding the plate of brownies in her other arm. His nephew clapped his hands and made gleeful noises as he and Martha finally cornered the goat and sheep. Diving for the lamb, Eli grabbed the animal while Martha caught the goat and fell to her knees to attain a better grip.

His breath came in harsh, rapid spurts, but Eli felt invigorated. He couldn't remember the last time he'd enjoyed a good run. As he studied Martha, he noted her disheveled appearance. He knew that he looked no better. His lips twitched, but Eli managed to control the urge to laugh.

"We should move slowly," Martha whispered, as if speaking in a loud tone would cause the goat to escape from her arms.

He nodded. "Wouldn't want one of 'em to get away," he agreed softly.

"*Ja.* You want to go first or shall I?" She looked young and approachable with her white *kapp* slightly askew and grass stains on her matching cape and apron. The goat began to struggle in earnest, and Martha shifted to get a firmer grip. "Why don't you head toward the barn first?"

"*Oll recht,*" he said, eyeing her with concern. "Are you sure you'll be able to hold her?"

She beamed at him. "*Ja.* I've got her *gut* now. I'm not about to let her go."

Eli inhaled sharply. He gazed at her, entranced. The widow was breathtaking when she was happy. Since her husband's death, Martha had been quiet, reserved. She'd been sad and grief-stricken whenever he'd caught a glimpse of her during church and on visiting Sundays. But during the past hour, she'd smiled and laughed... and looked like the happy young woman she'd been on the day she'd married Ike King.

Martha frowned, and Eli realized that he'd been staring. He quickly picked up the lamb and carried the frightened animal across the yard and into the barn. He gently placed it in the stall with its sibling. Then he returned to assist Martha with the goat.

His gaze quickly sought her as Eli stepped out into the bright sunshine. The animal was trying to chew Martha's *kapp* strings. Martha shifted the goat to keep the strings out of its reach. "Fence first?" he asked. "Or goat?"

She didn't hesitate. "Fence. I can hold her awhile longer, and I don't want any of the other animals to get out."

There were cattle and other sheep grazing in the distance. Eli went to the fence and quickly made a repair. Then he returned to carefully lift the goat from her arms and set the animal inside the secured pasture. Martha stood and brushed dirt and bits of grass from the hem of her skirt and her apron as he rejoined her.

Smiling, he shook his head. "I don't think you'll be able to get out the stains without a washing."

She flashed him a rueful smile. *"Ja."* She fell into step with him and they headed toward Annie and EJ. *"Danki* for your help."

"My pleasure. I enjoyed it." He felt his heart thump hard as they locked gazes. Startled, he quickly refocused his attention on his sister-in-law. "Annie, Jacob or Peter will come for you later."

Annie nodded, then released EJ, who stumbled toward him on unsteady legs. Eli swung the boy high and then into his arms. "I have to leave, buddy. Your uncle Noah needs me for deliveries. He's probably wondering where I am."

"I'm sorry." Martha looked apologetic. "I've kept you from your work."

"It was worth it," he assured her and meant it. "I needed the exercise." And he'd enjoyed seeing this other side of Ike King's widow. He grinned. "I haven't had this much fun in years." He gave his nephew a hug, then set him down. "Be a *gut* boy for your *mudder*." He laughed when the child beamed an innocent smile at him.

Annie caught her son's hand and drew him tenderly to her side. "Jacob will be disappointed that he missed the chase."

Eli shrugged. "I think we did well considering. Don't you, Martha?" He studied her, saw her smile and nod. "And Jacob would have been thick in the middle of it with us if he'd been here."

Martha lifted a hand to straighten her head covering, but her hairpins had shifted, making it impossible for her to fix it. "Would you like something to drink before you go?"

"Nay. I appreciate the offer." He stifled the urge to help Martha with her *kapp*. He grabbed his hat from the front seat of the wagon, finger-

combed his hair and put his hat back on his head. He became conscious of Annie's regard.

"What exactly did Noah want you to do today?" Her blue eyes twinkled as she studied him.

"I'll be making deliveries for him." Eli groaned and briefly closed his eyes as he realized that he was in no condition to greet Noah's customers.

His sister-in-law snickered. "Not looking as you do now." Her expression turned thoughtful. "You're not the same size as Noah, but I imagine he'll have clean clothes you can borrow."

"But will he have enough soap and water?" Eli heard Martha laugh as he climbed into the buggy. The sound rippled over him, making him smile.

"You can wash up in the house," she suggested. "I may be able to find something clean for you to wear." She paused when Annie whispered in her ear. Eyes widening, Martha gave a short gasp of laughter. "On second thought, maybe you should ask Noah."

"*Ja*, you'd best get moving, Eli," Annie urged. "It looks like you have your work cut out for you *before* you make deliveries." Laughter lurked in her blue eyes, and Eli scowled playfully at her.

"*Danki*, Eli," Martha said. "I couldn't have caught them without your help."

"You would have eventually," Eli said, "but

I'm glad I was able to assist." He readjusted his hat before he reached for the leathers. "It may be a *gut* idea to have your fence checked." He gave them each a nod. "Martha. Annie. Have a *gut* day."

With a click of his tongue and a flick of the leathers, he drove the vehicle toward the main road. A quick glance back showed him that Martha watched his departure. He smiled. The widow lingered in his thoughts as Eli pulled into the graveled lot next to his brother's furniture shop. He tied his mare to the hitching post and turned as Noah exited the building.

"Where've you been?" Noah asked as Eli approached. His brother gaped at him as they drew closer. "What happened to you?"

Eli removed his hat to run a hand through his hair. "I took Annie to Martha King's for Jacob."

"You had an accident!" Noah gasped, eyeing him with concern. "Annie—is she all right?"

"*Ja*, she is fine. But there was no accident. I had a run-in with two sheep, a cow and a goat." He chuckled at his brother's puzzled look. "I helped Martha with escaped livestock."

"And you got to looking this way how?"

Eli smiled crookedly. "They're wily critters. The cow wasn't hard to corner, but Martha's two sheep and goat were too cunning. Martha fared worse than me." He felt his mouth twitch before he allowed laughter to escape. "I actually enjoyed the chase. But I'm afraid I can't make deliveries looking like this." He gestured at his clothing. "Do you have a clean shirt and pants I can borrow?"

"Ja." Noah gazed at him with twinkling brown eyes that held mischief. "Rachel will enjoy a *gut* laugh when she sees you."

Eli gave him a sour look. "I'm not going to the house. If you don't care how I look, then I don't."

His brother's amusement faded. Noah sighed. "They're on the wall hook near the sink."

"Danki." Eli washed his face, neck and hands in the back room; then he dried his face with a clean towel from a stack on the shelf above the sink. As he changed his clothes, he thought of Martha. He envisioned her with her hair neat under a freshly laundered *kapp*. He imagined her wearing a purple dress with a clean black work apron. He smiled as he pulled the stopper on the sink and the water drained while he hung the towel to dry.

He rejoined Noah in the front room. "Better?"

"Better than what?" Noah joked. "The pants are a little short, but they'll do. No one will notice but me."

"Then I'm presentable enough for deliveries."

"As *gut* as you can be," his brother teased.

Eli snarled at him playfully. "Then let's get to work. Do you have a list?"

"Ja." Noah gave him a sheet of paper. As Noah explained about the pieces for delivery, Eli found his mind wandering…back to the King farm and the woman whose laughter had delighted him while lighting up her features.

"Eli! Pay attention!" his brother said sharply. "Did you hit your head while you were chasing animals?"

Eli thought of the impact of Martha's smile. "Something like that," he murmured before he made an effort to focus on work.

"I'd have loved to join the chase," Annie admitted as she followed Martha into the farmhouse.

Martha picked up EJ to carry him inside. "It was fun, but I'm glad it's over and they're penned up again." She smiled at the child's resemblance to Eli. "It was exhausting—I was at it for a while before you and Eli came. Thank the Lord you did, or I'd still be chasing them."

"I wish I had your energy," Annie said with a sigh. "Lately I've been too tired to do much of anything. This little one here—" She gestured toward her son. "He keeps me busy. I'm glad it's late April and the weather is finally warming again. I'll have to take EJ outside to play often. Maybe he'll tire himself out in the fresh air. Then I can have a long lie-down while he takes his nap."

"'Tis wonderful to get out of the house, *ja*?"

Annie eased herself down onto a kitchen chair and gestured for Martha to set EJ on the floor beside her. She regarded her son with tender warmth. "*Ja*. It was a long winter. Especially for you." She watched her son as he sat quietly and stared up at his mother. "He's being a *gut* boy. Do *ya* have a pan or pot he can play with?"

"*Ja*, in the cupboard." Martha opened a door and took out two pans along with a big metal stockpot. Then she dug into a drawer for wooden and metal spoons.

"You may regret giving those to him," Annie warned as Martha placed the spoons inside the biggest pot and gently pushed it in the boy's direction.

The toddler immediately reached for the spoon and began to bang on the sides of the pot. "I see what you mean," Martha said with a laugh. Before EJ had a chance to protest, she switched the spoon for a plastic spatula. The child grinned at her happily, stuck the spatula in a pan and stirred it about.

"Have you started on your vegetable garden?" Annie asked conversationally when her son was settled.

"I worked up the soil, but I haven't decided what to plant. You?"

Annie's smile held regret. "No garden this year, I'm afraid." She patted her pregnant belly. "I can't bend to garden."

"I'll put it in for you," Martha offered.

"You're a *gut* friend, but I can't let you do that."

"Then I'll bring you vegetables from mine," Martha insisted and was pleased when Annie didn't argue.

The women chatted and enjoyed tea while EJ played contently on the floor. Martha enjoyed the delightful morning spent in good company.

"What was all that whispering about?" Martha asked her friend as she had a surge of memory of Annie murmuring gibberish into her ear before instructing her to laugh, then encourage Eli to go to Noah's.

Annie grinned. "Do you know what it's like to be married to a twin? Eli is a consummate tease. I was just attempting to get one up on him."

Martha chuckled. "I see." She unwrapped Annie's brownies and poured EJ a glass of milk while the boy's mother encouraged him to climb onto her lap. Annie rewarded him with a cookie before she reached for a brownie.

Martha rejoined her friend at the table. A heavy knock resounded on her back door. "Who on earth…?" Answering it, she was startled to see her brother-in-law with three Lapp men—Samuel and his sons Jacob and Eli.

"Amos!" she exclaimed with surprise. "Is everything *oll recht*?"

"*Ja*, Martha, all is fine," her brother-in-law assured her. "We've come to discuss your farm."

An older version of her late husband, Amos wore wire-rimmed spectacles.

She allowed her gaze to stray briefly to the twins, especially Eli, who'd entered the house behind Amos and Samuel. Like the other men in the room, Eli had taken off his hat and held it. "I planned to seek your advice on who to hire to plant my fields."

With a smile for his wife, Jacob went to Annie's side and gathered EJ from her lap. The boy was happy to go to his father. Jacob smiled as he held his son close. "Martha, there's no need to hire workers. We'd like to do the planting for you." He hesitated before continuing. "We'll need seed. We can order it for you."

"'Tis already been bought." She felt uncomfortable being the focus of so much male attention. "After Ike purchased the new equipment, he ordered and paid for seed in advance. He mentioned that delivery would be this spring, but I have no idea when."

"Do you know where he bought it?" Eli asked, drawing her gaze.

"I have the receipt. I think he bought it from the same place as you, Amos." She'd found the receipt on the floor near her clothes chest recently. After its discovery, she'd been thankful that Ike had prepaid for the seed. She didn't know why he had, except that it might have had to do with his excitement over his new farm equipment.

"If you'll get it, I'll check on the delivery date for you. Will Wednesday of next week be *gut* for you?"

"But what of your own properties?" Martha was grateful for their help, but not at the risk of taking them from their own farmwork.

"We'll be done before then," Samuel assured her.

"Your help means a lot to me." She felt the onset of emotional tears and blinked to clear them.

Eli smiled. "Friends and family help each other."

The memory of his grimy face and dirty clothing as Eli had chased after her animals flashed into her mind. The pleasure from the image startled her. "I'll get the receipt," she said before she hurried upstairs to her old room. The bill of sale was right where she'd put it, inside the trunk near the foot of the bed she'd once shared with her husband. Then she returned quickly to the waiting men and handed Amos the receipt.

Her brother-in-law nodded with satisfaction as he studied it. *"Ja,* same place." He stuck the receipt into the crown of his hat. "I'll let you know what I find out."

Martha inclined her head. *"Danki."*

"Are you ready to go home?" Jacob asked his wife.

"Ja." Annie smiled at her handsome husband, who lovingly cradled their young sleepy son. She turned to Martha. "It's been a lovely day, Martha. Will you stop by our *haus* soon? We can visit while EJ naps," she said.

"I'd enjoy that," Martha agreed. "After the planting, if you're feeling up to it."

"I'll make dessert for Wednesday," Annie offered.

"No need. There will be more than enough food." She'd make sure of it.

Amos and Samuel put on their hats as they stepped outside. Martha followed more slowly with Annie and Jacob. She watched as Jacob, using one hand, helped Annie into their vehicle before he handed her their son. Amos and Samuel stopped to talk near their vehicles. Then Amos got into his buggy and left, while Samuel

Lapp waited by his vehicle as he looked back toward the house. "Martha, have you seen Eli?"

"Here, *Dat*," Eli's deep voice startled her from behind, causing her to spin to face him. "Martha."

"Eli! I didn't realize you were still inside."

"Annie forgot EJ's hat." He held up the child's small black-banded straw hat to show his father, and with a nod Samuel climbed into his vehicle.

Eli returned his attention to Martha. Her heart pounded as she gazed up at him. There was something about him with his golden locks, azure eyes and charming smile that did something strange to her insides. Alarmed by the feeling, she didn't smile back.

"If you need anything, just ask," Eli said. "All of us Lapps are handy with construction tools."

"That's kind of you." And it got Martha to thinking. The house needed repairs. Maybe after the planting she could hire the Lapps.

"Eli?" his father called through the open buggy window.

"Coming, *Dat*." He seemed reluctant to go. "It didn't take long to finish Noah's deliveries," he said as if she'd asked. "Some customers weren't at home. As you see, I found clean clothes." He started to cross the yard, then paused to grin back at her. "Don't be chasing livestock while I'm not here," he teased.

Martha had to smile. "I won't." Senses tingling, she watched as he climbed into his father's buggy and while they drove away from the farmhouse down her dirt lane. Eli Lapp was too charming, too handsome and too young— seven years younger—for her to give him another thought. She was getting ahead of herself. So what if she noticed an attractive man when she saw him? It didn't mean anything. She was still determined to remain single and manage on her own.

Chapter Three

Martha carried a large chocolate cake as she exited her farmhouse. She smiled at Meg Stoltzfus, who waited on the front porch.

"Let me," the girl said as she took the cake plate.

It was visiting Sunday. Meg, the young woman who'd stayed with her after Ike's death and through the winter, wanted to ride with her to the Samuel Lapps, their hosts. Meg often visited or attended church with her since moving back home. Despite their ten-year age difference, Martha and Meg had become good friends.

"How does your *vadder* feel about your riding with me again?" Martha asked as they headed toward her buggy. She didn't mind driving alone, but Meg wanted to come for reasons of her own, and Martha enjoyed the company.

Meg leaned inside Martha's vehicle and set

the cake on the back floor. She grinned as she straightened. "I enjoy the extra room. It feels crowded in the back of *Dat*'s buggy."

Martha approached the Stoltzfuses' carriage. "Morning, Arlin." She smiled. "Nice to see you again. Missy, you, too." Missy was Arlin's wife. "I hope you don't mind Meg coming with me again. She's a wonderful girl. I enjoy her company, especially after the winter I had." *After Ike's death.*

Arlin's stern, weathered face softened. "Staying with you was *gut* for her," he admitted.

Meg's four sisters were seated in the backseat of the vehicle. *"Hallo."* The girls returned her greeting.

"Dat, can I ride with Martha, too?" Charlie, named Charlotte at birth, was Meg's youngest sister. Charlie's nickname had worked out well since Martha's niece, who lived in Happiness, too, was also named Charlotte. The older Charlotte was happily married to Deacon Abram Peachy.

Arlin frowned while he seemed to struggle with his daughter's request.

"I don't mind if she rides with us, Arlin, but it's entirely up to you." Martha made the offer carefully; she didn't want to offend.

"Ja, Dat, it will be fun if Charlie rides with us." Meg beamed at him. "I promise we'll take

gut care of her. This afternoon we'll ride home with *you*."

Finally, Arlin gave a curt nod. *"Oll recht,"* he said, glancing back toward his youngest. "You may go with Martha and Meg." There were murmurs from the backseat as Charlie scrambled from the vehicle on her mother's side. He held up a hand. "Don't ask!" he warned his other daughters. "The rest of you will ride with your *mudder* and me this morning."

Ellie Stoltzfus leaned forward between her mother and father. "We are comfortable right here with you, *Dat.*"

The man's expression softened. "We should go," he said gruffly. "Katie will be wondering where we are."

Friends and families gathered to spend time with each other on visiting Sundays. Unlike church days when service started early, visiting occasions began leisurely with folks leaving for their destination midmorning. Martha enjoyed visiting family and friends.

"I'll follow you," Martha told Arlin, and the man nodded.

As Arlin steered the horse back toward the main road, Martha, Meg and Charlie climbed into Martha's vehicle, and Martha drove her horse to follow. The Lapp farm was on the opposite end of their village. As they drove past the William Mast property, Martha spied William and Josie approaching in their gray family buggy. "Morning, William. Josie," she called. She waved to the couple and their three children, who happily waved back. Martha continued to steer past Jacob and Annie's house, the Joseph Zook farm and Zook's Blacksmithy.

"Looks like Jacob and Annie may have already left," Meg commented. "I don't see anyone at their house."

"Ja," her sister said. Charlie leaned forward and gestured past Meg and Martha toward a residence on the left side of the road. "Look! There are Noah and Rachel. And their baby!"

Martha caught sight of Rachel and Noah exiting their house. "Noah! Rachel!" She slowed her buggy and waved.

The couple grinned and returned the wave. "Martha! Heading over to *Mam* and *Dat*'s?" Noah said as he cradled his daughter lovingly against his chest.

"*Ja.* 'Tis a great day for visiting."

"*Ja*, a fine one indeed," he called back pleasantly. "We'll see you when we get there."

"Who else do you think will be coming?" Meg asked as Martha drove on to catch up with Arlin.

"Not Reuben Miller, if that's why you're wondering," Charlie said. "*Ya* know he's not from our church district. Mostly likely, he'll be visiting his own friends and neighbors."

Meg got quiet. "I didn't ask about him."

Martha shot her a sympathetic look. "Have you seen him recently?" This past winter Martha had become Meg's confidante. She'd heard all about Meg's feelings for Reuben Miller, who had shown an interest in the girl last year at a youth singing. Reuben had sat across from Meg and paid her special attention during two additional singings, but then had become noticeably absent ever since. "Meg?"

"Nay." Meg kept her eyes on the road ahead. "It's been a while."

"The Zooks will be there," Charlie offered, obviously trying to cheer up her sister. "Peter should be with them."

"Peter." Meg groaned. "The last thing I need is *that boy* following me with those dark puppy dog eyes of his."

"Meg, what's the matter with you?" her sister exclaimed. "Peter is a nice boy, and he likes you." She sighed dramatically. "And he's so handsome."

"Too handsome for his own *gut,*" Meg replied irritably. She drew a sharp breath. "Reuben is nice and as handsome as Peter."

"I'm sure he is," Martha interjected. "But I imagine that your sister is concerned because

Reuben doesn't visit you as often as he should. Peter clearly likes you and wants nothing more than to make you happy." Directly ahead, Arlin slowed his horse, and Martha followed suit, pulling to rein her horse behind him. "I've never seen Peter bother you or be a nuisance to anyone."

Meg shrugged. "Just 'cause he keeps his distance doesn't mean he's not annoying," she said stiffly.

Martha stifled a smile. Meg always reacted strongly whenever Peter Zook's name was mentioned, a strange thing considering her claims that she harbored no feelings for him.

"Reuben's probably busy with farmwork," Meg offered.

"*Ja*, most likely," Charlie said softly as she leaned in her seat to be closer to Meg. "I only want you to be happy, Meg. I hope Reuben visits you soon since you like him so much."

Meg rewarded her with a smile. "I know you want me to be happy, Charlie. I want the same for you." She stayed silent a moment. "What if Reuben thinks I'm not interested in him? Maybe that's why he's stayed away."

Martha doubted it but kept her thoughts silent. "The Kinzer Fire Company Mud Sale is in June. So is the Lancaster County Carriage and

Antique Auction. Maybe you'll see Reuben at those events."

Mud sales were fundraising events exclusive to Lancaster County, where the Amish community helped to raise money for local fire departments. Each Saturday throughout the spring, members of their Happiness community donated craft and other items to be auctioned off to the highest bidder as well as food for sale for those attending the event. Mud sales got their name because typically the ground was muddy in the aftermath of spring rain showers when these sales or events took place. Those who attended mud sales frequently knew enough to bring their rain boots.

During the winter months, she and Meg had crocheted pot holders, sewn aprons and made other craft items for local mud sales. Most of their items would go to the two sales she had mentioned to Meg—the Kinzer Fire Company Mud Sale and the Lancaster County Carriage Auction—because they benefited the fire companies closest to their Happiness community. Every weekend through late winter and early spring there'd be other mud sales at different locations. There were also one or two that took place during August.

"He did tell me he'd worked as auctioneer

at the Kinzer Mud Sale two years ago," Meg said brightly.

Martha smiled as she continued to follow Arlin's vehicle as it turned onto the dirt road to the Samuel Lapp farm. "Then there's a *gut* chance you'll see him there."

"Look! There's Annie!" Charlie exclaimed as Martha parked her buggy in the side yard next to Arlin's vehicle. The girl waved vigorously through the side window. *"Annie!"*

Annie Lapp grinned as she saw them. Arlin and the rest of Meg's family got out of their vehicle, the girls quickly following their mother toward the house.

Martha caught sight of Eli Lapp surrounded by a laughing group of community girls. Clearly he was a favorite with them. Martha sighed. Had she been that carefree at their age?

She climbed down from her buggy, retrieved the chocolate cake from the back floor and followed Meg and Charlie to Annie's side. *"Hallo,* Annie," she said after the Stoltzfus sisters had greeted her good friend and moved on. "I'm glad you came."

"I'm feeling great today." Her friend lowered her voice. "EJ has been taking long naps, and I've been able to get some rest." The fact that the boy remained quiet and content within his mother's arms confirmed it. Annie's gaze settled on Martha's plastic cake tote. "Is that chocolate cake?"

"*Ja*, with dark fudge frosting."

"You better hide it from Noah. He loves anything chocolate." Annie smiled fondly at the mention of her brother-in-law's enthusiasm for chocolate. "He's liable to eat several slices before it's time to eat."

Martha chuckled at the idea of hiding her cake. "Is he that bad?"

"He doesn't just enjoy it," Annie told her. "He's obsessed with it."

Martha laughed outright. "Consider myself warned."

Rachel Lapp waved at them as her husband, Noah, drove past and parked in the line of vehicles. Meg and Charlie met the young couple, hoping to hold their baby daughter.

"Rachel is looking well," Martha commented as she watched Meg reach for baby Katherine. "Being a mother must agree with her." She smiled at Annie. "I know it does you."

"I'm feeling well and I'm happy. Jacob is excited about being a *vadder* again." Her friend's expression softened. "I'm afraid he expects us to have eight children like his *mudder*," she whispered with a laugh. "As if two *kinner* aren't enough to handle at the moment. He forgets that I'm not as young as his *mam* was when she had Jedidiah."

Martha eyed her friend warmly. "You want them, too." How she wished she could have had a family, but it wasn't meant to be.

"*Ja*, I do," Annie admitted with a chuckle. "We'll see what the Lord has in store for us."

A burst of laughter drew Martha's gaze once again toward Eli. The girls surrounding him were giggling at something he said, as he was grinning, obviously pleased with his audience.

"I wonder if Eli will ever settle down," Annie said.

Martha studied the young man objectively. "Those girls like him."

"And he enjoys their company, but never once has he shown serious interest in any one of them. Jacob says it's because Eli is determined to open his own business first. He's been working and saving for it for years."

"What kind of business?" Martha asked, more curious than she should be.

"A carriage shop."

"Here in Happiness?"

Annie shifted her son onto her other hip. "*Ja*. Says he wants to provide a service to our community."

Which said a lot about Eli Lapp, Martha thought as she watched him break from the group and head toward Noah and Jacob, who had stopped to talk near the barn.

Rachel approached with Meg and Charlie, who was now holding the baby. As they joined them, talk became centered on the infant.

"She's the sweetest baby," Charlie said as she studied the child in her arms, drawing a smile from little Katy's mother.

"She's growing too quickly," Rachel said.

"*Ja*, it can seem that way," Annie agreed. Her son wiggled within her arms, and she set him on his feet. "Stay here, EJ." She kept a firm eye on him. "Every time I see him it seems as if he's grown another half inch."

The women laughed. "Do you know how much a half inch is?" Meg Stoltzfus said. She showed the group with the space between her two fingers. "I wonder how you can tell EJ's size, as active as he is. He barely stays still."

"Except when he's asleep," Annie pointed out. She reached to grab hold of her son's hand to keep him close.

"A *mudder* can see the changes," Missy Stoltzfus said, joining the women in time to overhear her daughter and Annie's conversation. She had returned from inside the house.

"I'm glad you agree." She flashed Meg a teasing look.

Katie exited the house and approached. "What

a lovely day! Do you think the boys will want to play ball?" She reached down to run her fingers through her grandson's baby-fine blond hair.

"Peter will." Annie smiled at her mother-in-law. "*Ach*, and here he comes now with my *mudder* and *vadder*." Horseshoe Joe had pulled his buggy into the yard and parked it next to Noah's.

"Your *dat* has been doing well since his accident," Martha said.

Annie beamed. "*Ja*, 'tis hard to believe that two years ago he was unable to walk after he fell from his ladder."

"We've had much to be thankful for," Katie agreed.

"How are Josiah and Nancy?" Missy asked referring to Annie's older brother and his wife, Nancy, who was Martha's niece.

Josiah Zook had married Amos and Mae King's daughter Nancy last year.

"They are doing well." Annie picked up her son, who squirmed and tried to get away. "EJ, be still."

"I've never seen Nancy happier," Rachel said of her cousin.

Martha knew that Rachel had lived with her King relatives when she'd first arrived in Happiness. The schoolteacher's cottage had been under construction back then. Once the house was complete, Rachel had moved from her aunt and uncle's into her new home. Noah had been one of the men who'd worked on the teacher's house. After Rachel and Noah had wed, they'd lived in the cottage until a new house could be constructed for them elsewhere.

Peter stood chatting with a group of young Amish men near the buggies. Martha eyed him a moment and turned to study Meg, who seemed annoyed by the young man. Anne's younger brother broke away from his friends to saunter in their direction. He smiled when he saw EJ in his sister's arms. "I'll take him," he offered as he reached for his nephew, who was clearly happy to see him.

Annie smiled gratefully as she handed off her son. "He's a bit of a handful today."

"He's fine," Peter said with a smile for the child. "He'll be a *gut* boy for his *onkel* Peter, *ja?*" He casually glanced in Meg's direction. "*Hallo*, Meg. You're looking well."

Meg narrowed her gaze. "Peter," she acknowledged stiffly. When he looked back to EJ and walked away, the young woman appeared miffed that he hadn't paid her more attention.

Martha hid a smile. She had felt the increasing tension between Peter and her young friend. *Meg doesn't know it yet, but she may be sweet on him.*

"Let's go inside, *ja?*" Katie suggested. "'Tis

a nice day but not as warm as I'd thought. May I help carry anything?"

Martha shook her head when Katie offered to take her chocolate cake. "I can manage." She grinned. "I hear I should keep careful watch over this cake. Apparently there is someone in your family who may try to steal a piece before we're ready to serve it."

Katie laughed. "*Ja*, Noah, for certain. I'm afraid that most of my boys are partial to chocolate cake." She smiled. "Except for Jed. Jed prefers Sarah's cherry pie."

Martha accompanied the ladies toward the house. Eli and Jacob came up from behind them. The twins were deep in conversation, oblivious to the women before them. She saw Eli nudge his brother's arm with his elbow as he murmured something in Jacob's ear. The two brothers laughed, the sound deep, masculine and joyful. Martha turned and found that she couldn't tear her gaze from them as they drew closer to the women.

Suddenly as if he sensed his wife's presence, Jacob glanced in her direction, his gaze brightening as it settled on his wife. He gave her a special smile. "Annie."

"Jacob." She nodded solemnly. "Gossiping again?"

He blinked as if taken aback. "*Nay*, I—

we're—" He apparently saw Annie's smile because his lips curved up as he closed the short distance between them. "Trying to start trouble, wife?"

Annie blinked up at him innocently. "*Nay,* husband. I wouldn't start trouble. 'Tis not the Lord's way."

Martha heard Jacob's answering chuckle. She witnessed the couple exchange loving looks, and she wondered what it would have been like if Ike had cared for her as much as Jacob loved Annie.

An odd tingling started at her nape and traveled the length of her spine. Martha inhaled sharply when she realized Eli Lapp was staring at her. She experienced the urge to look away but didn't. As their gazes locked and held, Martha heard Annie and Jacob talking, but their words were lost on her.

"Eli. Jacob. Would you bring out the other table?" Katie called.

"*Ja, Mam.*" Eli broke eye contact as he and Jacob continued past them to climb the porch steps. The memory of his expression made it difficult for her to concentrate…and to breathe.

Martha and Katie followed the twin brothers into the house, while Rachel went to have a word with her husband. Missy and her daughters stayed behind and continued to chat with Annie and her mother, Miriam, along with Alta

Hershberger, who just had arrived. Martha tried to force her reaction to Eli from her mind as she entered Katie's kitchen, and she was successful until he and Jacob came out from another room carrying a small table. Then he was gone, and she could breathe again. "There is a lot of food, Katie," she said with a smile.

"Plenty enough for all of us," the woman agreed.

Martha wondered where she should put her cake plate as she looked over the kitchen countertop and trestle table.

"Chocolate?" Eli asked, startling her as he came up from behind.

She gave a nod but didn't turn around until he added teasingly, "Quick, hide it. Noah's coming." She faced him and immediately noted his sparkling blue eyes and the way his male lips curved upward.

Her face warmed as she felt an instant attraction. She didn't know whether it was his good humor or his teasing that appealed to her. Martha grinned, taken again by this playful side of him. "And you think I should give you the cake?"

"I can hide it for you." He gave her a mock frown. "Don't you trust me?"

"Should I?" He amused her.

"*Ja*, you can trust me." His voice was soft and

her nape tickled again as she found herself doing just that. She handed him the cake. "I'll put it in the back room," he whispered.

She inclined her head. They heard Noah and Rachel as they entered the house. Eli slipped into the backroom while Martha stayed as Katie greeted the couple and smiled at her grandchild.

"Here's my little *grossdochter*!" She beamed at the infant. "May I hold her?" She held out her hands.

Noah smiled as he handed the child to his mother. "Katy is a *gut* girl, *Grossmudder*. She slept until after seven this morning."

"Wonderful!" her grandmother exclaimed as she held the baby close.

As Eli returned from the back room, Martha felt a little jolt in her midsection the moment his intense blue gaze sought and met hers. "Safe and sound," he mouthed, causing her to smile.

Noah sniffed the air. "Do I smell chocolate?"

Martha regarded Eli with raised eyebrows before she went to check where he had put the cake—on the washing machine. He must have taken a peek beneath the plastic covering, as the scent of chocolate permeated heavily in the air and had filtered into the kitchen.

"It looks delicious," a male voice murmured in her ear.

"Eli!" she gasped and turned, her heart beating wildly. "You startled me."

His eyes twinkled. "I couldn't resist taking a look, but I didn't touch it."

She narrowed her gaze as she saw his expectant expression. "And now you want a piece," she guessed.

His handsome mouth curved into a grin. *"Ja."*

"I shouldn't give you one." She sighed dramatically, but she wasn't really upset. She was pleased that he was eager to try it. "I may as well bring it into the kitchen. There's no hiding it from your *bruder* now."

Eli looked delighted. "Then I may have a piece now?"

Martha chuckled as she picked up the cake and carried it into the other room. "One. You may have one slice." She grabbed a knife from among the utensils on the table. She sliced a piece, set it on a plate and gave it to him.

"Danki," he whispered, beaming.

"Do I get one, too?" Noah eyed Eli's cake plate with a hungry look.

"Ja, of course. Big piece or little?"

"Bigger than Eli's." He flashed Eli a grin and then watched eagerly as she served him a slice of cake. His warm brown eyes gleamed with appreciation as he cut a mouthful with his fork and raised it to his lips. "I love chocolate."

Martha smiled. "I never would have guessed."

Eli beamed at her. "We all do."

"Ja," Noah said as he raised a forkful to his mouth.

"Noah Jeremiah Lapp!" his wife scolded. Rachel winked as Noah stiffened before turning to her with a guilty look.

"Cake before dinner?" Rachel said with hands on her hips.

His expression warmed as he stepped closer. "It's chocolate."

Her brow cleared. "Ah, I didn't realize. I certainly can't have you missing out on a piece. After all, it may be all gone if you wait until after you've eaten a proper meal."

She laughed when Noah blushed.

"It could be all gone," Eli defended as he and Martha exchanged amused glances. He dipped his fork into the cake, brought it to his lips.

Martha couldn't seem to take her eyes off him. "I should have brought two." She covered the cake with the plastic lid. "Time to put it away before there's none left."

"Gut idea," Rachel said after she and Martha had shared a smile. When Noah was finished, she grabbed hold of his arm. "We need to go outside."

"Eli? Are you coming outside?" a young voice called into the house.

Eli smiled at Mary Peachey as the young woman entered the room. "Soon," he told her. He didn't leave immediately but continued to eat his cake. "That was delicious," he declared after he'd eaten his last bite. Unlike Noah, who had rushed through his piece, Eli had savored every bite slowly.

"I'm glad you enjoyed it," she said.

"I wouldn't mind a second helping, but I won't ask," he added quickly when he saw her disapproval.

"Gut," she replied, trying hard not to be persuaded by his little boy smile.

He shrugged. "I should go." He paused to study her a long moment. *"Danki* for the cake."

"You're welcome." She turned to search for Katie.

"Mam's outside," he said as if he'd read her mind.

Turning from his appreciative look, Martha refused to be charmed like the young girls who waited for him. She continued to feel his gaze on her as she crossed the yard to join Katie, Rachel and the other women who had gathered on the back lawn.

She knew the exact moment when he rejoined his friends. The girlish laughter that immediately came from the group at his arrival grated in her ears. Martha frowned. Why would she care who he spent his time with?

He took that moment to lock gazes with her. A small teasing smile played about his lips, making her heart race despite the fact that she didn't want to notice or feel the slight hitch in her breathing.

"You can bring chocolate cake anytime," he mouthed. A young girl drew his attention, and Martha looked away.

She had to admit that Eli was both handsome and kind, and if she'd been younger, never married and had never suffered a broken heart, she might have felt differently. Like the giggling girls across the yard, she might have welcomed the man's attention. But she wasn't young and she wasn't looking for another husband or beau of any age.

Twice men had disappointed her. She wouldn't allow one to disappoint her a third time. Especially a man like Elijah Lapp.

Chapter Four

Martha enjoyed a pleasant visiting Sunday before heading home after the midday meal. It had been nice to see her friends. Watching the Lapps with their extended family, she'd felt the love and the joy that filled their lives.

She regretted not having a family of her own, one that she'd never have now that Ike was dead. There were times she'd wanted to see her parents and siblings, but they rarely ventured from Indiana and had come to visit only once, for her wedding. She had no intention of visiting her childhood home. There were memories there, hurtful memories. It was there that her sweetheart had asked her to marry him...before he'd changed his mind and chosen to leave their Amish life for the English world.

She loved her Happiness community. The people here had welcomed her with open arms from the first. They were always available for whatever she needed. She had made many friends, and her brother-in-law, Amos, his wife, Mae, and their children were her family. While she wished she could see her *mam*, *dat*, her *bruder*, Micah, and sister, Ruth, she knew that this was where she belonged. She had married Ike and made this community her home. Why would she want to leave? It had taken Ike some time to ask to court her and then become his bride. They had been seeing each other for months at community gatherings before he'd made his intentions known.

As she steered her horse onto her dirt driveway, Martha recalled how nervous Ike had been on the day he'd asked her to be his bride. Once news reached the church community that he finally had popped the question, no one had seemed surprised.

"Took him long enough," Mae had said. "But don't *ya* fret, Martha—Ike will be a *gut* husband. I know he thinks highly of you. He's been working up the nerve to ask you." The fact that Ike had discussed her with his family was unusual, as courting was done discreetly and never discussed outside the involved couple until it became serious when the banns were read in church.

Hearing news of the impending marriage,

Annie had confided to Martha that she'd wondered what had taken him so long to propose. Everyone had noticed the way Ike had followed Martha with his gaze at community gatherings.

Before the wedding, gossip about Ike's earlier interest in Annie had caused Martha moments of unease. Since Annie was her closest friend, Martha had gone to her for the truth.

"*Ja*, he asked to court me," Annie had said, "but not because he cared for me. He simply assumed that I'd grab my last chance for a husband." Her friend had eyed her with concern. "Martha, you've nothing to worry about. Ike didn't love me. His wife had passed on just a short time before he moved back to Happiness. He never once looked at me the way he looks at you. I have to admit I did give marrying him some thought, but only because I was determined to steer clear of young attractive men like Jacob. I'd had my heart broken by Jedidiah, and I wasn't looking to get hurt again. Jacob loved me, and I fell in love with him, too."

"You were meant to be together," Martha had agreed with a smile.

"I didn't even have to tell Ike. His interest had turned elsewhere." She'd regarded Martha with warmth. "He'd met you."

The day of their wedding was the happiest day of her life. Their first seven months of marriage had been wonderful; she was in love with her new husband, who was kind and attentive. Later, after he'd become disappointed that she hadn't conceived, Ike had changed. He no longer paid her much attention. He'd spent all of his time on farmwork and looking for new farm equipment. She'd been upset when the shiny new equipment had arrived, but she'd kept silent. She couldn't have stopped him from making the purchase. He was in charge of the farm and she the house. If her husband could afford it, why shouldn't he have the best tools?

The men were coming to her farm for the spring planting on Wednesday. They would have a chance to use Ike's equipment then. She had food to prepare and the house to clean. Meg, Charlie and Nell Stoltzfus would arrive tomorrow morning to help her get ready for the workers.

As she'd exited her buggy and approached the house, she couldn't help but notice, as she had many times, the repairs that were needed to the farmhouse. Despite her gentle requests to fix things, Ike had turned a blind eye to the problems. He had bought this farm with its large English farmhouse incomplete. It must have used a lot of her late husband's money and time to finish the house enough to live in it. He had grown tired of working on it or had stopped caring about needed repairs.

"I own the house free and clear, Martha," he'd told her on the day she'd agreed to be his wife. "The house wasn't finished, but I got it done and did most of the work myself. I paid someone to do the plumbing."

Martha had stared at the brick house and thought it sturdy but too big.

"Someday we'll have children to fill the bedrooms," he'd told her.

Martha had blushed. That was a lot of bedrooms to fill, and she wasn't a teenager with years ahead of her to have that many babies.

"*Ya* do want *kinner*?" Ike had asked, watching her closely.

Martha had nodded. "I love *kinner*." And he'd looked relieved.

"We will be happy together, Martha." His smile had been warm, and she'd felt loved. But there had been no babies during their time as man and wife.

Ike was a good man. She missed him, but she wondered how their relationship would have fared with no children. She'd been deeply hurt by his change in behavior, as if he'd believed that she'd defied him on purpose by not getting pregnant. As if it hadn't been *Gottes wille*.

We married for better or worse. Ike had been

an active member of the Amish church. If he'd loved her, her husband would have accepted their marriage and their life together with or without children.

Martha sighed. She had to stop thinking about what should have been instead of what was.

"I will manage," she murmured as she entered the big empty house alone. Ike had left her a nice nest egg, which would tide her over for several months. If the farm produced well this season, then she would be set for another year. She was glad that the property was paid for and the only thing she needed to be concerned about were life's basics and whatever she needed to keep up with the farm. She needed to fix the things that Ike had ignored, for she could ignore them no longer. She knew that the Lapp men did carpentry work for the community. She could hire them to do the repair work.

Monday morning, Martha was cleaning the kitchen after breakfast when the Stoltzfus sisters arrived. She'd baked earlier and set out a plate. "Muffins?" she asked.

"We ate before we came," Meg said. "Perhaps later with tea after we're done?"

Martha smiled. "I made blueberry, chocolate chip and sweet."

"I wouldn't mind one now," Charlie said.

When Meg looked at her, the girl blinked. "What? I didn't eat much breakfast."

"Tea, anyone?" Martha asked.

"Nay." Charlie happily took a bite. "May I have some water?"

"I'll have a cup of tea." Nell, the eldest sister, came in from the outside. "I went to check on your animals," she told Martha. "They look well. Have you given thought to selling any of your baby goats?"

Martha shook her head. *"Nay.* Do you know someone who is interested?"

"Ja, me."

"Nell, what will *Dat* think if you come home with another animal?" Meg asked with a shake of her head.

"He'll think it a *gut* idea," Nell assured her. "Martha, I'd like a female if you're willing to part with it. Think about it and name your price. Then let me know. *Ja?"*

"Nell loves animals and is always looking to add to our livestock." Charlie took a sip from the water Martha had given her and set the glass down.

"I'll think about it," Martha said. She owned several goats. She probably could part with one or two.

Katie Lapp and Martha's sister-in-law Mae arrived next. "I didn't expect you to come," Martha said with surprise as she held open the door for them.

Katie smiled as she entered. "We wanted to help."

Mae followed Katie inside with a pie plate in her arms. "*Snitz* pie," she declared.

Martha grinned as she accepted it. "Sounds delicious. *Danki*, Mae."

The women dispersed to different rooms to give the house a thorough cleaning. Martha was a good housekeeper, so the work didn't take long.

When they were done, the women gathered in Martha's kitchen for refreshments. Martha made tea and coffee and set out the *Snitz* pie and the plateful of muffins and another dish of homemade cookies. As they ate, they caught up on community news and then left before early afternoon.

Martha needed to buy groceries to fix Wednesday's food. She decided to make a quick stop on her way to the market to check on her friend Annie.

"Martha, what a pleasant surprise!"

"I wasn't sure if you'd be resting." She'd brought the last of the *Snitz* pie and made Annie up a basket of baked goods.

Her friend smiled. "EJ finally fell asleep, and I've just put on the tea kettle. Would you like a cup?"

"*Nay*, I should go so that you can have some quiet time and rest." The teakettle whistled, and she insisted on making Annie's tea. "After your baby's born, I'll come to help." She would live to enjoy others' children since she couldn't have any of her own.

Annie blinked against tears. "You're a true friend, Martha. I'll keep that in mind."

"*Gut*." Warmed by their friendship, Martha cut Annie a slice of *Snitz* pie. "I have a few things to be repaired at the house."

"How many things?"

Martha grimaced. "A lot."

"Jacob's father and *bruders* are fine carpenters. They built this *haus*."

"I remember. I thought about asking them, but I know they're busy with farmwork. Do you think they'll agree to take a look when they have time?"

"*Ja*. I'm sure they will." She leaned back in her chair and placed a hand on her pregnant belly. "If the others are otherwise engaged, Eli can do your repairs. He takes on extra work wherever he can find it."

Her heart skipped a beat at the memory of Eli Lapp's teasing grin. "To save money for his carriage shop," she murmured.

"*Ja*. I told you about that, didn't I?"

Martha nodded. "Would you like me to check on EJ before I go?"

"Would you?" Her friend appeared grateful, and Martha headed upstairs to the child's bedroom. EJ slept with his legs curled beneath him with his little derriere pointed upward. She could see his sweet face; the little boy looked vulnerable and adorable. And he made Martha long for a baby of her own. She returned to the kitchen and her friend. "He's still napping."

"I love to watch him sleep," Annie admitted. She started to rise.

"Sit," Martha ordered gently. "You don't look well."

"I'm fine."

But she didn't look fine to Martha. Annie looked exhausted and uncomfortable, seated at the kitchen table with her eyes closed.

"Shall I get Jacob for you?"

Annie blinked her eyelids open. "*Nay*, he has too much to do today." There was love in her gaze and deep affection in her tone.

"Stay home Wednesday, Annie." Martha filled the dish basin in the sink, then collected her friend's cups and plates.

"You don't have to wash those."

Martha turned to her with raised eyebrows. "*Ja*, I do. You've been a *gut* friend to me, Annie. It's the least I can do." She dried and put away the dishes. When she was done, she saw that her friend had fallen asleep in the kitchen chair.

"Annie," Martha whispered, touching her shoulder lightly. "Let me help you to bed. You should lie down before EJ wakes up."

Annie nodded and pushed back her chair. Martha took hold of her arm and Annie leaned against her as Martha walked her to her bedroom and helped her into bed. "I'll come back to check on you later."

Annie had already closed her eyes. "No need. Jacob said that he would be home early."

"Rest. I shouldn't have stopped." Martha placed the small quilt at the end of the bed over Annie.

"Nay," her friend murmured. "I enjoyed your company."

EJ's bedroom was in the next room. If the toddler woke up, his mother would hear him. "I'll lock the doors on my way out."

"Danki," Anne whispered.

As she stepped outside, Martha was surprised to see Jacob and Eli ending a discussion. Jacob headed toward Zook's Blacksmithy while Eli walked to his vehicle with a tool belt draped over his arm. She was surprised to see his buggy alongside hers.

As if sensing her presence, Eli glanced in her direction. "Martha," he greeted her with a respectful nod. "I didn't expect to see you here today."

"Eli." She couldn't help notice that the blue of his eyes matched the azure sky above. "Just stopped to check on Annie. Mae made *Snitz* pie, and I thought to share it."

He smiled. "That was kind of you."

"Annie is my friend."

"Still I'm sure she appreciated your thoughtfulness." He reached up as if to climb into his vehicle.

"May I speak with you?" Martha asked before she could change her mind. It was the perfect opportunity to see if he was interested in doing her house repairs.

"Ja." He faced her with eyes filled with curiosity.

"I know that you, your *vadder* and your *bruders* are skilled carpenters. I'd like to hire you to do some work on my *haus*, if you're interested." She didn't know why she suddenly felt jittery inside. She would have to get used to hiring people and taking care of the things that her late husband had handled in the past.

His blue gaze brightened. She saw that she'd piqued his interest. "We can stop by if you'd like," he said pleasantly. "Give you an estimate."

She felt relieved. "That would be wonderful. *Danki.*"

"May we come tomorrow?" he asked when she turned to leave.

Martha faced him. "Morning?"

His expression filled with warmth. "What time?"

"Come anytime. I'll be there all morning." She felt her heart beating wildly as she turned back to her buggy and reached for a handhold. Eli was suddenly beside her, silently offering his assistance. Their gazes locked. His features held only polite indifference. Relieved, she allowed him to help her into her vehicle. After he released her fingers, she could still feel the warmth of his firm, gentle grasp. She opened her mouth but was suddenly at a loss for words.

"I'll see you tomorrow, Martha."

She didn't answer him, which bothered her as she sat a moment and watched while he sprang up into his wagon. Their gazes met, held, until he touched the brim of his hat and dipped his head.

Martha watched him leave before she followed the same path toward the road. The memory of their brief encounter stayed with her as she drove toward the market, while she shopped, paid for her groceries, then drove home.

Later that evening she scolded herself for worrying needlessly about her reaction to Eli Lapp.

She finally put things into perspective. He was her friend's son, and he'd been kind to her. Gratitude. That was all it was.

Chapter Five

❧

The next morning Eli sat next to his father as he steered their buggy toward Martha's farmhouse. As he'd suspected, *Dat* was pleased to do the work for the widow. "Amos is worried about her," he'd said when Eli had first mentioned it to him. "He knew that his *bruder* had ignored the *haus* repairs. I imagine that Martha has been wanting things fixed for some time."

"Then 'tis *gut* that we can help her," Eli had said, and his father had agreed.

It was a warm and sunny day. Spring flowers had burst into bloom, adding a splash of color to the houses built along the main roadway. Residents, both English and Amish, were outside tending to chores in their yards or on their farms.

Eli and his father lifted a hand in greeting to Abram Peachy, church deacon and friend, who was driving his buggy in the opposite direction.

"Abram," *Dat* greeted him as their vehicles drew abreast of each other. "Nice to see you on a fine day such as this."

"Should have more of the same tomorrow," Abram said. "'Twill be a *gut* planting day for Martha's."

"*Ja*, you'll be there then?" *Dat* asked.

Abram bobbed his head. "*Ja, ja.* Wouldn't miss it. Martha's family."

"We will see you tomorrow, Abram," *Dat* said, and they went their separate ways.

They rode in silence until they reached the King property. As *Dat* steered the horse into the widow's driveway, Eli spied Martha in the backyard hanging laundry.

She glanced back as if sensing their presence and waved.

"She knows we're here." Eli watched as she stopped what she was doing and approached with a smile.

"Martha," his father greeted her as he climbed from the vehicle.

"Samuel." She gave him a nod. Her gaze slid in his direction. "Eli."

"*Hallo*, Martha." She looked well, he thought. The fresh air and spring warmth clearly agreed with her.

"You're out early this morning," she said.

"Is this a bad time?" Samuel asked.

She shook her head. "*Nay*, this is the *gut* time. It's kind of you to come."

"Do you have a list of what you want done or would you prefer to show us?" Eli felt himself the focus of her brown gaze. His thoughts flashed back to her seated on the ground, laughing, after one of her escaped animals got the better of her.

"I'd prefer to show you."

Dat indicated his pad and pencil. "I'll make a list."

"If you follow me, we'll start around front."

Eli trailed behind as Martha and his father discussed the areas of the house that needed their attention—and there were a lot of them, too many for him to remember. Fortunately, his father took notes as Martha explained what needed to be done. Eli found his thoughts wandering to the tiny dark tendrils of hair at her nape below her *kapp*.

"Eli."

He shook himself from his thoughts. *"Ja, Dat?"*

"Can you start work next week?"

"Ja, I'm available." Eli allowed his gaze to shift again to Martha. He was charmed to see her suddenly pink cheeks, and he smiled. He turned to his father. "Monday?"

Dat looked up as he closed his notepad. *"Ja.*

That will give us Thursday to take another look around to see exactly what materials we need."

"And you'll write up a proposal?" Martha asked.

"*Ja*, I'll check on some prices and let you know." His father paused, and his smile for her was reassuring. "Amos and I have been friends and neighbors nearly all of our lives. You can trust us to do a *gut* job for a reasonable price."

Martha's expression warmed. "I know," she said without hesitation.

Captivated by her features, Eli stared for a moment until she glanced his way, and he quickly averted his gaze.

"We should get home, *soohn*," Dat said.

"*Ja*. It will be suppertime before we know it."

"You just ate lunch," his father reminded him.

"And carrot cake," Eli said with a laugh. "With chocolate chips. I'm hoping for another piece."

He felt Martha's gaze and experienced a kick to his stomach at the amused look in her brown eyes. "What can I say?" he told her. "I like sweets."

"*Ja*, I gathered that."

Dat adjusted his hat. "Martha, we'll see you soon."

Martha nodded her thanks. "I appreciate your help."

"Our pleasure," his father said.

Eli was aware of her as she walked them to their buggy.

"Martha, may I take a quick look inside the barn?" *Dat* eyed the structure across the yard.

"*Ja*, feel free," she said.

And then Eli found himself alone with her as his father headed toward the outbuilding. He watched *Dat* disappear inside the barn before he turned to the woman beside him. The silence between them seemed charged.

"Looks like the *gut* weather will hold for to-morrow's planting," he said conversationally. Martha nodded. Eli became more aware of her during the ensuing silence. "No critters in your yard."

His comment made her smile, as if she enjoyed the memory of the chase. "*Nay.* Thanks be to *Gott.*"

She was beautiful when she smiled, Eli realized. Her whole face lit up, and the brightness was reflected in her warm brown eyes. "If any of them get out, you know where to find me."

She laughed. "If I can leave them alone long enough to get you." Today, she looked lovely in a dress in spring green with matching cape and apron. Except for those small hairs at the back of her neck that he'd noticed earlier, her dark hair was rolled, pinned and tucked up neatly beneath her white head covering.

He liked standing beside her, wished there was more time for them to have a conversation. Eli was curious about her, her family back in Indiana, about her marriage to Ike. He furrowed his brow. Not that he'd ever ask.

He took off his hat and brushed a hand across his nape before he put his hat back on. As their gazes collided, she quickly averted her glance. He became intrigued about why she seemed embarrassed to be caught looking at him.

His father reappeared, drawing their attention. "I didn't find anything useful," *Dat* said with regret as he rejoined them. "Not to worry, though. We'll get what we need in town."

"*Danki*, Samuel."

"We haven't done anything yet."

Her smile was rich and warm. "*Ja*, you have."

Samuel flipped open his pad and jotted down some more notes. "Time to go," he said when he was done.

Eli nodded. "We'll see *ya* tomorrow, Martha." He looked forward to tomorrow's farmwork. He skirted the buggy to climb into the passenger side.

"Would you take lead?" his father said off-handedly as he flipped open his notepad.

"*Ja.*" He climbed into the driver's seat as his father got in on the other side. "Have a *gut* day, Martha."

"You, too, Eli. Samuel. Have a blessed day."

Eli clicked his tongue, flicked the reins and drove their vehicle toward home. He really was looking forward to tomorrow's farmwork. *Because most of the community will be there to help out.* He enjoyed working beside his father, brothers, and neighbors. Hard work. Delicious food and the satisfaction of putting in a full day's work. It had nothing to do with the fact that the farm belonged to Martha King.

Chapter Six

❧

Wednesday morning, Martha woke before dawn. The community men were coming to plant her fields today, and there was much for her to do to get ready. She dressed and then set up a food table on the back lawn. It was a cool early May morning, but she couldn't have asked for nicer weather. She returned to the house and put on the coffeepot. While the coffee perked, she unwrapped muffins, coffee cake and the fresh bread she'd made yesterday. She then pulled out coffee mugs with fixings and debated whether to cook eggs now or closer to the workers' arrival time. After the coffee had perked, she transferred the fragrant brew from the pot to a thermal decanter. Then she set about to make a second pot. When the coffee was ready, she brought the cups, coffee decanter and a thermos of hot water for tea outside.

Most but not all of the church community men
would come to help out. Among the workers
would be her relatives, the Amos Kings, all of
the Samuel Lapps, the William Masts and the
Abram Peachys. Mentally calculating to make
sure she'd made enough food, Martha smiled.
She always enjoyed spending time with family
and friends, and the people coming were among
her favorites.

The Samuel Lapps arrived first, just as the
light of dawn brightened the sky. Samuel parked
his buggy and climbed out, followed by his sons
Isaac, Daniel and Joseph. Katie stepped out of
the passenger side, followed by Hannah, the couple's youngest child. But there was no sign of Eli.

Amos and Mae arrived soon afterward with
their two sons, John and Joshua. Amos would be
trying out Ike's new farm equipment today, and
Martha detected a hint of excitement among the
men. Jacob Lapp came next with a small plow in
the back of Horseshoe Joe's wagon. Peter Zook
rode in the front seat beside him.

Martha managed to stifle a frown. There was
still no sign of Eli.

Smiling, Katie approached with her daughter.
"Guder Marriye!"

Martha's lips curved in response. "And a fine
day to you, Katie." She beamed at the woman's
daughter. *"Hallo*, Hannah." A delicious scent

wafted from the food dish in Katie's arms. "You've brought breakfast."

"*Ja*, egg casserole with sausage and potatoes," Katie said. "Hannah, would you please put this dish on the table? Be careful. It's still hot." She handed her daughter the dish, which was wrapped in a heavy bath towel.

"Sounds wonderful." Martha watched Hannah hurry to the food table and set down the casserole dish. The girl placed it beside a plate of muffins, then scurried back to her mother's side.

Martha felt her gaze drawn to Samuel and Jacob, who, together with Peter Zook, hefted a small plow from the back of Horseshoe Joe's wagon and set it safely on the ground. When they were done, Jacob headed in the women's direction. "I understand we'll have a lot of help today."

Katie nodded. "*Ja*, my husband and sons and many more." She smiled as Jacob reached them. "How's Annie?"

"Tired and at home, I'm afraid." Jacob looked apologetic as he met Martha's gaze. "She wanted to come, but—"

"I told her to stay home and rest," Martha interjected with a smile and saw his relief.

"Jacob, where's Eli?" Hannah asked her big brother.

"He'll be along." He gestured toward the end

of the dirt driveway. "Look!" Eli had made the turn from the paved road onto her farm property. He was riding on the back of a large plow drawn by two draft horses.

Martha watched with an odd feeling in the pit of her stomach at the sight of him. As if realizing that he was being watched, he halted, grinned at them, then took off his straw hat and waved with it.

"He's a tease," his mother said fondly.

"He's a *gut* man," Jacob reminded her, and Katie agreed with a silent nod. "Those are Joe's horses and plow. Joe asked if he would help, and Eli would never say no to a friend who asked a favor of him."

The blond man, who was the topic of discussion, settled his hat back on his head and drove the plow into the barnyard. Martha watched as Jacob met his twin brother.

"I thought you'd never get here, *bruder*," Jacob teased as Eli climbed down from his seat.

"*Ya* think it easy to be driving down the street when there's traffic?" Eli shuddered. "I worried that a speeding car would spook the horses and they'd drag me down the road never to be seen or heard from again."

Peter gave a bark of laughter. "Those two? Not likely. Those horses are as tame as they get."

"Have you ever steered along a busy road?"

Eli asked, eyeing Annie's brother beneath lowered lids. "And if so, why didn't you bring them yourself?"

Peter shrugged. "I figured you'd do a better job of it."

Eli's lips twitched as if he hid a smile. "You can take them back later today. See how you like it."

"Maybe," Peter said noncommittally.

Martha was concerned about Eli's frightening tale of large farm machines on busy roadways until she saw the twinkle in Eli's eyes as she encountered his glance when Peter turned away.

Arlin Stoltzfus came, accompanied by his daughters, Meg and Charlie. The two young women joined Martha, Katie, Mae and Hannah in the yard not far from the food table.

"*Dat* said we didn't have to come, but we wanted to visit," Meg confessed to Martha.

"I'm glad you did. Come inside. We'll put on a pot of tea, if you'd prefer, and sit until we're needed to serve lunch or for sowing seed."

"We're nearly done," Jacob said.

Walking beside the horses while his brother was behind the plow, Eli pulled off his hat to wipe his brow with his shirtsleeve. "I don't know about you, but I'm hungry."

"I could eat something," Jacob admitted. "It seems a long time since breakfast."

"Martha made muffins and bread," Eli pointed out as he continued to maneuver the horse into the field row. Mention of Martha brought back the memory of her smiling face. "And *Mam* brought an egg casserole."

"I wasn't hungry earlier." Jacob handled the plow with the efficiency of years of experience learned at his father's side.

"You're usually always hungry," Eli teased him as Jacob often did him. He loved his twin and was amazed how much alike they were in thought if not in physical features. Jacob had dark hair like their father and Jedidiah. He, their younger brother Daniel and their little sister Hannah had golden-blond hair, while their other siblings, Noah, Isaac and Joseph, had hair like their mother's in varying degrees of sandy blond and brown.

"How's Annie?" Eli wasn't surprised that his sister-in-law hadn't come. In her advancing pregnancy, she'd become more tired than usual. Caring for a twelve-month-old didn't help her situation. Eli was actually surprised when Jacob had stopped by the house yesterday to ask him to drive Joe's plow. Eli had agreed because he knew his father would have enough help with his brothers.

"Annie wanted to come, but I convinced her to stay home. She is exhausted. Miriam is minding EJ at the house so Annie can rest. *Grossmama* is happy to help as she gets to spend time with her beloved *gross soohn.*"

"You are a fortunate man, *bruder.* You have a woman who loves you, a precious son and another one on the way."

Jacob smiled. "Someday you'll find the woman you're meant to marry *and* the life you want for yourself."

"No time to think of marriage now. I need to open my carriage shop first."

"You'll open it. As hard as you've been working, you'll have it within the few months, I'm sure."

"I'd like to believe that."

"Noah said you've been looking for a place."

Eli nodded. "*Ja.* He thought I had enough to get started, but I don't know yet where to search. Noah said he'd help me find a good location."

"You'll figure out where. The Lord will guide you." Jacob became thoughtful. "Eli, the Lord blessed me with Annie, and I've never been happier or more at peace."

"Time will tell what the Lord wants for me." *Time and prayer*, he thought.

They worked each field row until they'd reached the end of their assigned area. "Let's head back," Eli suggested. On their return to the barnyard, he spotted Amos seated on his late brother's shiny new plow, his sons, John and Joshua, walked alongside him.

"Appears Amos is done, too," Jacob commented.

Eli saw his father with Isaac and Daniel, who had also finished plowing. It hadn't taken the three teams long to work up the soil on Martha's farm.

"What do you suppose is for lunch?" Jacob asked seriously.

"Food," Eli declared, making his twin laugh. "And that's *gut* enough for me."

Martha watched as the work crews returned to the barnyard. "That didn't take long," she said as she pulled the plastic cover off a bowl of macaroni salad.

"There isn't a farm in all of Happiness that can't be plowed within a few hours when there are three crews doing the work." Meg came to stand at Martha's side.

"Do we have everything we need?" The young woman nodded. Martha asked, "Do you think they're hungry?"

Meg chuckled. "Does a cow moo? *Ja*, they'll be hungry. They're men with healthy appetites, and they haven't eaten in what—four *whole* hours?"

Charlie exited the house, carrying two pitchers of fresh homemade lemonade. "Where would you like these?" she asked.

Martha gestured toward the end of the table. She frowned. "Or do you think we should set up the drinks on a separate table?"

"*Nay.* There's room here," Meg said.

"The iced tea is ready, too. I'll get it." Charlie, a pretty girl with red hair, freckles and green eyes, returned to the house for the iced tea. She came back within seconds. Martha watched her approach. The girl's dress was light green, a color that heightened her eye color. Like her sister Meg, Charlie was always ready to lend a helping hand.

Martha gave her a smile of thanks as Amos, his sons and Annie's brother Peter headed in their direction; they were the first workers to come looking for food. "Amos, how's the new plow?"

"*Gut.*" Amos looked pleased. "Your horses drove it well."

"'Tis much nicer than my *dat*'s plow," Peter said.

"Your *vadder*'s equipment does the job well enough," Amos reminded him. "Look! Here come Jacob and Eli. They've finished as fast as we did."

Peter frowned as he adjusted his hat brim as

if to shade his eyes from the sun as he stared at the twin brothers. "But the newer plow does a better job than the old ones."

"'Tis not the equipment that matters, Peter," Katie offered. "It's the one who does the work and does it well."

Meg firmed her lips. "*Ja*, Peter, why should you care what kind of plow your *vadder* uses?" she said sharply. "The one he owns does the work just fine."

At Meg's sharp words, a shutter came down over Peter's expression. Martha felt sorry for the young man. Peter wasn't envious over Ike's farm equipment. He was simply impressed by the new machinery, of which he'd never before seen the likes.

"Meg," she warned, and Meg had the good grace to redden. Didn't the girl realize that she had the power to hurt him deeply? It was obvious that Peter cared for her.

"What's to eat?" Eli asked, breaking the tension as he approached with Jacob.

"Eli!" his mother scolded.

"What? I can't ask about the lunch menu?"

Martha laughed out loud. "Food," she said. "It's on the table. You'll have to look for yourself."

Eli rewarded her with a dazzling smile before

he hurried over to do just that. His "Looking *gut*!" made Martha chuckle again.

"I don't know about that one *soohn* of mine," Katie said.

"Two *soohns*." Jacob grinned at his mother. "I was about to ask the same thing."

Martha eyed him with amusement. "And I'd have given you the same answer."

"The two of you are so much alike in some regards 'tis almost frightening." Katie shook her head. Jacob went to join Eli near the food.

"Those boys," Katie said, her lips curving into a reluctant smile.

"You are blessed to have such wonderful *soohns*." Martha watched as the brothers circled the table and pointed out their favorite foods.

"*Ja, Endie* Katie," Meg said. "My cousins are *gut* people."

"That doesn't mean they don't worry their *mudder*."

"Why?" Martha asked, curious. From what she knew of the Lapp brothers, they were good men who loved their mother, their families and God, but not in that order. "Why do you worry about them?"

"Every one of my children has given me cause for concern over the years."

"You can't protect them, but you'd like to," Martha said with understanding. She had prayed for the opportunity to become a parent, but the Lord had chosen other plans for her.

"Ja," Katie said. "Fortunately, my three oldest are happily married to their wives."

Martha studied the men in question—Jacob and Noah...and Jedidiah, who had just arrived to help out. "The Lord has blessed them."

"Ja," Katie said softly. "He did."

For the next hour, the women served food to the workers. As Meg, Charlie and Katie filled plates, Martha checked to ensure there was plenty of food for everyone. Some of the dishes were disappearing fast. She went inside to refill platters and bowls and plates. After setting them on the food table, she returned to the house again to fetch two of the four cakes she'd baked yesterday. Martha saw the men eyeing them appreciatively as she set them on the table and uncovered them.

"Cake," Eli said, sniffing appreciatively. He was the first in line for a slice of Martha's mint chocolate-chip cake.

The other workers followed suit and came to wait for their share.

After the men had filled their bellies, Martha watched as the crews went back to work. Their next job would be to cultivate the soil to ensure the ground was soft enough for seed. They might till the fields many times, if needed, to prepare the dirt properly.

Martha found her gaze drawn to Eli as he and Jacob switched places behind Ike's new cultivator. He appeared to enjoy working with the equipment while, walking along beside him, Jacob helped steer the horses and remove any obstacles, such as rocks and other debris loosened by the machine blades.

Eli had pulled his straw hat low to shield his eyes from the sun. A light breeze rustled his royal-blue shirt and dark pants as he rose on the horse-drawn machinery from one end of the field to the other.

She smiled as she switched her attention to Annie's husband. Jacob was a good man who loved his wife. Annie had made a wise choice when she'd married him.

Her thoughts turned naturally to her late husband. She was sincerely sorry that Ike had died without the joy of holding his own child. Martha tried to imagine him as a father of a houseful of children, but for some reason she couldn't. Would he have been capable of tenderness toward his children, or would he have become impatient when the reality didn't fit his imagination?

Jacob Lapp was tender to EJ, and he didn't mind showing it. Noah was sweet and loving toward his baby daughter. Was it a mother's influence on her sons that had made them such good husbands and fathers, unashamed of showing affection?

Ike had been gruff; she'd wondered since his passing if he would have been the father he'd hoped to be.

"Martha?" Eli's voice startled her later that afternoon as she cut up the second cake and transferred the slices to small paper plates. Earlier she'd made fresh iced tea, and Meg and Charlie had carried out more lemonade as well as chilled bottles of pop.

"Back so soon?" Martha felt her face heat as she met Eli's smiling gaze. "Are you here for another piece?" His regard made her feel tingly. "Is something wrong?" she asked when he hadn't replied.

He shook his head as he continued to study her. "I'd like to try the lemonade." He watched her as she reached for the pitcher, poured him a glass. "We're getting ready to sow seed," he said.

Martha gave a start. How long had she been lost in her own thoughts? "We are?"

"Amos and my *dat* are still cultivating, but they'll be done soon." He directed her attention to the horse-drawn machinery he'd recently driven. "That machine can do six rows at a time. Makes the job easier."

Martha, recalling Ike's claim, nodded. "He said the new equipment would cut farmwork time in half."

"It does." Eli continued to gaze at her with piercing blue eyes. Her face warmed. "As for the sowing—I don't mean we as in you or any of the women, but us men." He pointed out another of Ike's machines. "A planting machine. Does the work in less than half the time as sowing seed by hand."

She was impressed and told him so.

"We'll be starting your repairs on Monday," he reminded her. "*Dat* will stop by tomorrow with your estimate."

"I appreciate your help." She stopped her fingers from playing with the edge of her apron.

"I should get back to work." He glanced toward the barn, where Jacob had hitched up the draft horses to another of Ike's shiny new machines. "We'll finish up today. If not, we'll be back tomorrow morning."

Martha was grateful for the help from her friends and her new family. Katie and Hannah happily helped in the kitchen, while Meg and Charlie carried dishes to and from the food table and kept watch for workers who stopped in for a quick drink or snack. The men toiled until the sun began to set in the west; then they finally came in from the fields to pack up for home.

While his sons lifted the single row plow and set it carefully in the back of their wagon, Samuel approached Martha, who chatted with his wife.

"Got most of it today. We'll finish up first thing tomorrow." Samuel looked warm, his shirt moist against his skin. He had worn a long-sleeved shirt along with navy tri-blend pants and work boots, and the day had turned hotter than expected. The breeze had ceased that afternoon, and while the humidity wasn't bad, Martha realized how hot it must have felt to the men doing her farming.

"*Danki*, Samuel," she said gratefully. "I can't tell you how much I appreciate your hard work."

He smiled. "'Twas our pleasure, Martha. Eli and Isaac will be back early tomorrow morning. I've checked on material for your repairs, and I'll get you a proposal by tomorrow afternoon. On Monday, we'll get started if everything meets with your approval."

"Martha," Mae interrupted as she approached from behind. "Amos is ready to leave. You will let us know if there is anything you need?"

"You've done more than enough." She looked around gratefully at everyone within sight. "All of you." She released a breath. "*Danki*. If there is anything that I can do for you, any way to repay you—"

Samuel frowned. "There will be no repayment."

"Cake!" Eli called out at the same time.

Martha looked at his teasing grin and cracked a smile. His father stared at his son, and the innocent look on Eli's face had Samuel shaking his head with amusement.

"Done!" Martha said before anyone could object. "I just happen to have an extra cake or two in the house. If you'll wait just a moment, I'll get them."

Katie spoke up. "Martha, there's no need—"

"I know, but 'tis my pleasure," Martha called back as she hurried toward the house. "I baked too many, and I can't eat them all!" She had seen the pleased gleam in Eli's blue gaze when she mentioned the extra cake.

Feeling unusually lighthearted, Martha grabbed the cake, then returned to hand it to Katie. "Eli will ruin his supper if he gets a hold of this," she warned.

Katie's lips twitched. "*Ja*, he probably will." She turned to her son. "Do you hear that, Eli?"

"But *Mam*—"

"Time to go, *soohn*," his father said. "Be happy you have a cake to enjoy after dinner."

Martha choked back a chuckle when she saw amusement twinkling in Eli's expression. "*Danki* for the cake, Martha," he said solemnly. "I'll eat it after supper."

Martha burst out laughing. "You're not fooling me, Elijah Lapp." Jacob approached from the yard, and she offered him the last cake to take home to Annie.

His brown eyes lit up. "She'd like that."

She retrieved the other one and gave it to Jacob.

The workers and their families left, and Martha was alone in the house as light darkened into night. As she prepared for bed, she thought of the day and how grateful she felt for the help and the friendship of her church community. She thought of all the work done by her family, friends and neighbors. Katie Lapp and Missy Stoltzfus had cleaned up her kitchen and left it spotless.

Next year I'll pay someone to work. Her mind found an image of Eli Lapp. He was strong, healthy and a good farmer. Perhaps she could hire Eli and his brothers to plant for her next season. She'd have to give it some thought. She frowned as she had trouble banishing from her thoughts Eli Lapp with his warm, teasing demeanor.

Chapter Seven

"Do you have everything?" Samuel placed his tool belt into the back of the wagon.

"*Ja, Dat*. We have the tools we need and the two-by-fours you picked up on Friday." Eli studied the sky. "The day looks to be a *gut* one, so we should get a fair amount of work done today on Martha's farmhouse."

Isaac left the house and joined them. "Jedidiah coming?" he asked as he placed his tool belt next to *Dat*'s.

Dat nodded. "*Ja*, he said he'd come for a while this morning. We'll work on the windows after he gets there."

Eli climbed onto the front wagon seat, while his father climbed in on the passenger side. Isaac jumped into the back.

The air was clean and fresh, filled with the scents of *Mam*'s roses, as Eli steered their mare down the dirt lane toward the main road. Janey was in good form as she pulled their vehicle onto the King farm. Jedidiah was waiting for them in Martha's barnyard as Eli parked their buggy next to Jed's. He got out of the vehicle. "*Hallo*, Jed."

"Took *ya* long enough, Eli," Jedidiah teased.

"You could have come with us," Isaac suggested as he climbed out of the back.

Jed shook his head. "I can work this morning. Have other work to do this afternoon." He smiled as his father left the vehicle to join them. "*Gut* to see you, *Dat*."

Their father was pleased. "Ready to get started?"

"*Ja*. Sarah fed me an early breakfast."

Eli reached into the back of the wagon for the tools he'd need. "What did you have?" All of his sisters-in-law, like his mother, were wonderful cooks.

"Cinnamon rolls." Jedidiah's gaze grew soft. "But she made me eat eggs first. Said the sweet rolls alone wouldn't keep me going until lunch."

"I would have liked a cinnamon roll." Isaac grabbed the tool belt Jacob had given him and strapped it on.

His father raised his eyebrows. "Your *mam* made you a fine breakfast."

Isaac shrugged. "I still would have liked a cinnamon bun."

Jedidiah laughed. "I'll ask Sarah to wrap one up for you."

"How are Sarah and Gideon?" Eli opened the back of the wagon and slid out several two-by-fours, which he stacked near the barn. Sarah and Annie had given birth within three months of each other. Annie and Jacob had welcomed EJ, his namesake, after Sarah and Jedidiah had been overjoyed with the new arrival of their son, Gideon.

Jedidiah smiled. "They are doing well…wonderful."

Eli had never seen Jedidiah this happy before he married Sarah Mast from Kent County, Delaware. They'd met at Spence's Bazaar and Auction in Dover. Jed had accompanied their uncle Arlin to sell Arlin's wooden craft items and their mother's herb, vegetable and flower plants at the flea market there. Sarah had been selling baked goods. It'd been a chance meeting between the two young people when Sarah's young brothers had chased a puppy into a busy parking lot and Jed had rescued the boys from being hit by a car. It seemed as if God had devised a plan for Jed and Sarah when they'd encountered each other again in Lancaster County at the home of William and Josie Mast, Sarah's cousins, who were the Lapps' neighbors and friends. But Sarah's mother's health had been an obstacle to their future happiness until Ruth Mast had made a full recovery after heart surgery. Daniel and Ruth Mast had encouraged their daughter Sarah to follow her heart and begin a life with Jedidiah in Happiness.

Seeing his brothers happy with their chosen wives made Eli long for a love like theirs and a family of his own.

"The windows along the back are the worst," *Dat* said, interrupting Eli's thoughts. "We'll start with those."

Jedidiah frowned. "Why do any windows need to be replaced? Didn't Ike just buy the place?"

"Five years ago. The windows were installed before Ike bought the farm," *Dat* explained. "He left them in although the weather had taken a toll on them long before he purchased the property. And he didn't paint them, which made matters worse."

Jed examined a lower-level window with peeling trim. "These are going to take some work."

Eli, who followed with Isaac, answered, "*Ja,* but we'll get it done." *What had Ike been thinking to ignore needed repairs to the house yet buy new farm equipment?*

"Eli, why don't you let Martha know that we're here?" *Dat* said. "Isaac, Jed, grab the lumber Eli unloaded."

"Ja, Dat," Isaac said as he moved to obey with Jed lending a hand.

Eli knocked softly on Martha's back door. It was early, and he hoped that she was awake. Most women in his Amish community were up at dawn or before, but Martha was a widow who lived alone. Her work and sleep schedule might be different.

When she didn't appear after several moments, he knocked a little louder. This time the door opened immediately. Drying her hands on a kitchen towel, Martha appeared unsurprised to see him. "Eli," she greeted him. "Ready for work?"

"Ja, we'll be at the back of the house this morning." He studied her, noting how her blue dress complemented her dark hair and brown eyes.

Martha flipped the towel over her left shoulder. "The windows?" He nodded. *"Gut."*

They gazed at each other for several seconds until Martha seemed suddenly eager to do her chores.

"Try not to worry," he found himself saying as he backed up to go.

Her lips curved. "I'm not worried. I know I hired the right crew."

Eli returned her smile. "We'll try not to make too much noise."

"You'll have to use a hammer, *ja*? Make whatever noise you need to get the job done."

"As if we can help it," he teased. He left with the mental image of her bright brown gaze and warm smile. His father and brothers were discussing where to start when he rejoined them. "Martha knows we're here."

"Gut." His *dat* eyed the back of the house. "Jedidiah, let's start with the second-story windows."

"Ja, Dat." Jedidiah put the ladder against the house, then tested to see if it would hold.

"The windows are scheduled for first delivery." He pulled a pencil from behind his ear and jotted notes onto a clipboard. "They should be here at any time. Isaac, I'd like you to scrape the paint peeling off the window trim. Start with those on the back side."

Isaac grabbed a paint scraper and went to work. Eli figured that he'd be sanding that same trim.

The truck from the local lumber company arrived with the ordered windows. The loud *beep beep* of the delivery truck as it backed into the barnyard drew Martha to the back door to learn the cause of the commotion. When she saw the truck's company logo, she went back inside and closed the door.

Eli signed for the window and gave the delivery slip to his father. He then grabbed sandpaper and joined Isaac at the opposite side of the house from the dirt drive.

"I don't understand," Isaac said. "Wasn't the house finished a couple of years ago?"

"*Ja*, Ike must have been short on funds that he didn't finish the house properly." Eli folded the sandpaper and began to sand an area Isaac had completed.

"So now Martha bears the expense of fixing them," Isaac said.

"*Ja,*" Eli said. He felt bad for Ike King's widow. Ike had found the money to purchase new farm equipment, but he'd ignored the problems with the farmhouse. She couldn't have been happy about it.

By midmorning, Isaac and he had scraped and sanded all the side lower-level windows. Jedidiah and their father had cut the shipping straps off all of the windows after checking to see that each one was the correct size. There had been no sign of Martha since the window delivery. She didn't come out to check on their work.

"Eli!" *Dat* called. "We need your help over here!"

"Coming, *Dat*!" Eli rounded the house to find that Jedidiah had climbed up the ladder to the second floor to size up the window situation and decide how best to proceed. Eli took over steadying the ladder from his father, who went inside the house to speak with Martha. Jed climbed down, and when he reached the bottom rungs, Eli stepped away.

"Best to work from inside," his brother said, and Eli agreed.

Dat returned from talking with Martha. "Go ahead inside, Jed. Martha understands that we'll need access to the rooms upstairs."

Jed picked up a window and carried it inside. He appeared within minutes at the second-story window he'd examined earlier.

"Take another window up to Jed," *Dat* said.

Eli obeyed, excusing himself to Martha as he passed her in the hall. It felt awkward for him to walk through her home without an invitation, even though she'd requested the work.

By noon, they had removed and installed three windows and were discussing a plan to install more tomorrow.

Martha brought them sandwiches and drinks for lunch. "I hope you like chicken salad."

His mother had made ham sandwiches for them before they'd left the house, but Eli didn't want to hurt Martha's feelings when she went to all the trouble. "I love chicken salad," he said truthfully.

She looked pleased. "Would you rather eat them inside?"

"Nay," his father said. "We'll eat out here." He explained that they were too filthy to eat at her kitchen table.

The sun shone in a bright blue sky. A balmy breeze made it a good workday and provided the perfect weather for enjoying lunch on Martha's back stoop.

Martha gave them soap and towels, and the three of them—and Jed, who had to leave—took turns washing up at the hand pump. Jed left, and they sat down to enjoy Martha's food. The sandwiches were delicious and so were the potato chips she'd added to each plate. When they were done eating, Eli collected the dishes and took them inside. She answered his knock immediately.

"Danki." He smiled as he gave her the empty plates. "The sandwiches were delicious. You make a great chicken salad. The potato chips were a nice surprise."

"I'm glad you enjoyed them." She took the dishes from him and studied him a long moment. "Are you still hungry? Do you want dessert?"

He shook his head. "We need to get back to work," he said with regret.

She brought the dishes in the sink. "I'll fix you something different tomorrow."

Something softened inside of him. "You don't have to feed us, you know."

"I want to. It's nice to cook for someone other than myself."

"I can't speak for my *vadder* and *bruders*, but I'll be happy to eat whatever you want to make."

She seemed delighted. Her smile warmed him like a summer's sun. "Tomorrow I'll give you cookies instead of potato chips."

"I should get back to work." But he hesitated, wishing he could stay and talk with her awhile. He forced himself to turn.

Her soft voice stopped him. "Eli?"

He spun back. *"Ja?"* He eyed her curiously, wondering what she had to say.

She opened her mouth to say something and then closed it as if she'd changed her mind. She blinked. "Your *vadder* is behind you."

He turned. His father stood several yards away. Eli quickly approached him. "Was I taking too long?" he asked as he followed *Dat* back to the work area.

"Nay. I wanted to thank Martha for the food, but you already did," his father said approvingly, surprising him.

"Ja. Martha wants to feed us again tomorrow."

There was a sudden shift in his father's features from solemn to smiling. "It gives her pleasure."

Eli nodded. "Then we should tell *Mam* not to make our lunch tomorrow."

Samuel nodded. "*Ja*. If Martha wants to cook for us, we'll let her."

As he glanced back toward the house, Eli saw Martha in a downstairs window, but after their gazes met, she quickly disappeared from view.

The strange sounds from outside the house since early that morning were disconcerting. Except when she'd brought the Lapps a meal, Martha had stayed inside, unwilling to get in their way. She'd gone about her daily chores, working to clean the entire house from top to bottom, starting at first with the upstairs bedrooms, until she'd glimpsed a face in the window while dusting furniture. Startled, she'd gasped but managed not to scream. It had taken her only a moment to recognize Jedidiah Lapp as the man on the ladder. She'd scolded herself for being frightened. Fortunately, Jed hadn't seen her as she fled the room. She'd left to clean the rooms downstairs with a plan to finish the upstairs later. But as she'd swept floors and dusted furniture in the gathering room, she'd remained overly conscious of their masculine voices. Eli speaking with his younger brother Isaac. Samuel's voice joined with Jedidiah's as he called up to Jed at the top of the ladder. She'd frozen at hearing scraping sounds from the right side of the house.

What is wrong with me? I'm not usually this unsettled. She made a concentrated effort to relax and succeeded as she did her chores.

Late that afternoon Martha exited the house as the Lapps put away their tools. She studied the residence. "Looks like you got a lot done today, Samuel."

The older man beamed. "*Ja.* We replaced three of the upstairs windows and scraped and sanded several others on the main floor. Tomorrow we'll finish up the second story and then start on the ones up front." He skirted the vehicle and climbed into the passenger side.

"*Danki*, Samuel."

Eli didn't say a word but acknowledged her with a nod as he picked up the leathers. Martha returned to the house with mixed emotions. She was worried about the money she'd spent, but she was grateful that she had hired the right men for the job. The thing that most concerned her was that she'd found herself frequently searching through her windows for Eli Lapp throughout the day.

Chapter Eight

During the days that followed, Martha baked, cooked and did other chores while the Lapps worked on the repairs outside. Their time on the job took on a pattern. Each day the men arrived early to find that she'd left them muffins and bread along with a pot of coffee with fixings and mugs. Later she emerged from the house to pick up their empty dishes. At noon she brought them lunch, and in the afternoon she put out drinks and snacks. Samuel continued to tell her that she shouldn't go through the trouble, but much to her delight the man and his sons ate whatever she'd made for them.

It was a sunny and warm Friday. Eli and Isaac arrived earlier than usual. Birds chirped as they scattered about the lawn, stopping occasionally to dig for bugs and worms in the dirt. Martha knew of the Lapps' arrival before she heard Eli's knock. It was always Eli who came to see her first thing. Catching a glimpse of him through the window, she tapped on the glass to gain his attention. "I'll be right there."

He nodded, and when she opened the door, he smiled at her. "We're back. Just Isaac and me today."

Martha was glad to see him. "You're getting an early start. You must have things to do elsewhere." Given the price Samuel had given her, she worried whether he or Eli made enough money doing this job. She couldn't forget that he'd been working for his future carriage shop.

"*Nay.* Not today. Don't worry. We'll get your job done."

She averted her gaze from the warmth in his blue eyes. As Eli turned to leave, Martha burst out impulsively, "Do you like egg salad?"

He paused and looked at Isaac, who nodded. "*Ja*, we love egg salad."

"About noon?"

"We'll be hungry then," he said with a grin.

"Then I will see you at noon." She opened the door to enter the house but then halted to look back. "Let me know if I can get you anything before then." She hadn't expected them this early, so she'd yet to put out food for them.

"We had a *gut* breakfast," Eli assured her.

She nodded and went inside. His smile made her heart beat rapidly. She felt breathless… tingly…alive.

Eli was aware of the scent of Martha's knockout roses as he worked to remove the paint from the trim surrounding the front door. The red blossoms were growing on each side of the front steps. Every time the breeze blew, he got a whiff of their perfume and thought of Martha.

He took off his hat, set it on the steps and ran both hands over his scalp. Closing his eyes, he fought the images that constantly invaded his mind. *Martha chasing sheep. Martha seated on the ground laughing, dirty, appealing. Martha struggling to hold Millicent to keep the goat from escaping.*

The way she continually became the sole focus of his thoughts disturbed him. Eli fought to concentrate on the job. He wondered why Ike had used wooden trim instead of metal or vinyl. When he'd first heard of the work, he'd been happy to take the job because it meant earning money to add to his carriage shop funds. Now he was also glad to be helping Martha.

Eli paused to stretch before he went back to work. The old paint was coming off the wood nicely. He worked on the front door trim while Isaac did the same labor around the back door.

He stopped to check on his brother. They had been on opposite sides of the house for most of the morning.

"How are you managing?" he asked as he approached.

Isaac stopped and looked at him. *"Gut."*

He could see that his brother was doing a great job. "Nice work."

"Then let me get back to it," his brother said good-naturedly.

The back door opened suddenly, catching them both by surprise. Martha stuck her head in the opening. "Hungry yet?"

"Ja," Isaac said.

"Egg salad?" Eli pushed up the brim of his hat to better see her.

"With or without lettuce and tomato?"

"Lettuce and tomato," he and Isaac answered at the same time.

Martha disappeared into the kitchen, closing the door behind her. Through the window screen, they could hear her moving about as she made their lunch.

Within minutes, she had fixed their lunch, and to Eli's surprise, she invited them inside to eat.

"We're dirty from the work." Eli wanted nothing more than to sit at her table, but he felt too grimy.

Martha went back inside. "Brush off your

clothes," she said when she came back out with soap and towels. "Use the pump out back to wash up."

Eli nodded; he'd used the pump before. This time, since she'd invited then to her kitchen table, he took extra pains to wash thoroughly—and twice. He wet and lathered his hands and forearms with Martha's homemade scented soap. Then he rinsed them under the water that Isaac pumped out for him. "I need to wash my face, too," he told his brother. He took off his hat and put it out of the water's reach. Then he cupped his hands to capture the running water, splashed it on his face and across the back of his neck. He lathered both areas and rinsed them by sticking his head fully under the water. As the cold water washed over his head and neck, he laughed. He straightened, met Isaac's amused gaze and said, "Your turn." And he handled the pump as his brother washed up.

Martha stood at the door, studying them through narrowed eyes as they toweled themselves dry. "And do *ya* think you'll be coming into the house wet like a cat caught in a rain shower?"

Eli felt his face turn red. He'd wanted to be clean before entering her house; he'd never given any thought to what water would do to her floor and furniture.

"We'll eat out here." He looked away, stung by her scolding.

Martha grinned. "Both of you come inside. Can't *ya* tell when someone is teasing you?"

Eli widened his eyes, delighted. Some folks thought her plain, but he thought she was the prettiest girl he'd ever seen. Especially when her eyes sparkled as she smiled or laughed.

He dried his head and nape with the towel Martha gave him. The terry cloth smelled of laundry detergent and fresh air, a scent he imagined would be on all her linens and towels. He followed Isaac into the kitchen. "Do you have a couple of extra towels?" he asked when she came into the room from the front of the house.

"Ja." She appeared to be gauging how many towels they'd need. She disappeared into another area of the house and returned with a stack of blue folded terry cloth. "These should be enough."

Eli's lips twitched. "Appears to be." He took a towel from the pile for his brother and one for himself.

Martha watched them as they finished drying, then declared, *"Gut* enough." She gestured toward the kitchen table. "Come and sit."

Eli studied the two chairs that had been pulled out near place settings. Martha had set two towels on each of their chairs.

Eli stared at the towels. His lips curved as he captured Martha's gaze. "Are *ya* certain that you don't want to add another towel or two to our seats?" His hands and arms were dry. His hair was damp; his pants were bone-dry. Her decision to pad the chairs with this many towels amused him.

Martha opened her mouth, then shut it. To his surprise, she blushed. "Sit down and eat your lunch."

"*Ja*, Martha," Eli said at the same time as Isaac. Their chorused answer made them chuckle. Martha joined in and seemed happy to share a meal with them. When they were done eating, Eli reluctantly rose. He'd enjoyed eating in Martha's kitchen, watching as she and Isaac carried on a conversation while he listened quietly. "It's getting late. Time to get moving again." He glanced at her approvingly. "*Danki*, Martha."

Isaac thanked Martha and they went back to work. There was still much to do.

The afternoon went quickly. As he sanded the door frame and then put on a fresh coat of paint, Eli found his gaze straying toward Martha, who had come outside to work in her garden. He tried to concentrate on the job but found his attention drawn often toward Ike's widow.

"Eli." Isaac held the base of the ladder as Eli

carefully painted second-story window trim from an upper run.

Satisfied with his finished work, Eli climbed down until he was eye level with his brother. *"Ja?"*

"It's getting late. How much longer are you planning to stay?"

Eli glanced in Martha's direction. "We can leave. We've done enough. I'll tell Martha." He met her as she approached the house. "Martha, we're calling it a day."

Martha eyed Isaac's earlier handiwork, where he'd scraped and sanded around the back door. "Nice work," she said as Isaac joined them.

Isaac looked pleased. *"Danki.* Tomorrow I'll put on another coat of paint."

She seemed relaxed as they packed up their tools and stored them in the back of their wagon. "I'll see you in the morning."

Eli was overwhelmed with a sense of pleasure at the thought of returning the next day. *"Ja,* we'll see you then."

It was a beautiful morning. Martha had done on a load of wash at dawn and now she enjoyed the warmth of the sun as she pinned the garments to the clothesline. The Lapp brothers had been coming for more than a week now, and she expected them to arrive within the hour. The sound of an approaching horse-drawn vehicle caught her attention. She pinned the dress, left her laundry basket in the grass and went to meet the buggy driver, who had parked in her barnyard. To her surprise, Eli stepped out of vehicle and tied up his horse alone.

She blushed. The two-wheeled carriage he'd driven resembled the type used for courting. She pulled herself together. Eli didn't notice her approach; she was able to study him freely. Martha noted his tanned forearms below the sleeves of his maroon work shirt. He wore navy tri-blend trousers with black suspenders. He reached to retrieve his tool belt, and she caught a glimpse of his nape below his blond hair. He turned and grinned when he saw her standing within a few yards away.

"Martha! *Guder marriye!*" He looked glad to see her.

Martha's pulse started to thrum. "*Gut* morning, Eli. Working alone today?"

"*Ja.* Jedidiah had to work with Matt today. Isaac is helping *Dat* on the farm. Noah would have come, but he has an order to finish for Bob Whittier."

Bob Whittier, a local store owner, often helped members of their Amish community. He drove them whenever there was an emergency and frequently allowed them to use his phone free of charge for important calls.

"Why aren't you helping your *vadder*?"

"He says he doesn't need my help." Eli reached into the cart, picked up his hat and placed it on his head. "I'd rather be here." She caught the twinkle in his blue eyes. "You pay me to work." His smile held pure masculine appreciation.

She gasped. Was Eli flirting with her? She sighed, affected despite herself. The ability to flirt came to him naturally. She felt a pleasant prickling along her spine. She recalled him, grinning, laughing and surrounded by girls. He was a good-looking charmer, and she wasn't immune.

"What are you planning to do today?" she asked as he continued to smile at her. Butterflies fluttered in her belly, and she felt her cheeks warm. "Finish painting and few items on *Dat*'s list." He studied her for a long moment. His smile disappeared. "I'll get to work."

Martha wondered if she'd offended him as he walked away only to halt, glance briefly back and move on. She watched him as he headed to the barn and returned within minutes with a can of paint and other paint tools. He walked with bent head until he drew closer and glanced up. Martha went back to her basket of wet laundry.

As she pinned up some towels and a set of bed sheets, she flashed a look in Eli's direction.

What is it about this man that makes me unable to ignore him? A man who could have any girl he wanted—she had seen the proof of it last visiting Sunday. She recalled the two men who had hurt her and made her life difficult.

Not again. It wouldn't happen a third time. *Not with anyone.* She sighed and forced her attention back to hanging laundry, but she remained aware of the man working within several yards of her.

Chapter Nine

Eli poured white paint into a roller tray. Wetting the paint roller thoroughly, he began to white-wash over faded sections of the house's exterior. The weather was perfect. The sunshine felt warm, but the day's humidity was low. He frowned as he found his gaze straying frequently to Martha at the clothesline and then later in her vegetable garden. He had seen something in her eyes that had bothered him. Usually he enjoyed talking with her, teasing her, but this morning she hadn't seemed to appreciate his good humor. She'd withdrawn from their conversation until he'd figured he should get to work and leave.

Since starting this job, he'd woken up each morning eager to head back to her farm. He was glad to be earning money. But more than that, he liked knowing that he was doing something important for Martha. He didn't know why it gave him satisfaction, but it did.

He experienced an odd settling in the pit of his stomach as he studied her. She wore a black apron over a pink dress and a simple navy kerchief over her dark hair.

Had he said something to offend her? Was that why in the midst of their conversation she'd become distant, reserved?

She looked up suddenly as if she'd sensed him watching her. He glanced away, unwilling to be caught staring. He checked again and couldn't look away as she set down her spade and approached. Heat washed over him as she drew closer. He was embarrassed to be caught staring after their last encounter.

"I didn't realize it was so late," she said. "You must be hungry."

He was startled by the myriad of thoughts running through his head. "A little," he admitted.

"Do you like strawberry jam sandwiches?"

"I love strawberry jam," he said with a slow smile.

She returned his smile, and he felt instantly better than he had all morning. "Give me a minute to wash up and I'll fix lunch. I'll leave the soap and towel on the steps."

He watched as she entered the house, and he

carefully set his roller pan out of the sun. Then
he washed up at the pump.

A short time later, Martha appeared with two
sandwich plates. "Here we are." She moved toward the wooden bench on the edge of her garden, expecting him to follow. He did but was
slow to do so.

"I thought we'd eat here," she suggested as she
set down their plates in the middle of the bench.
"I'll get our drinks and be right back."

"Do you want me to get them for you?"

She shook her head. Eli watched as she entered the house and returned with lemonade. She
handed him the two glasses. He placed them
carefully on the ground within easy reach, and
then he took a bite of his sandwich. A wild burst
of strawberry flavor burst into his mouth complemented by Martha's tasty homemade bread.
He eyed her to gauge her mood. He felt that
she was relaxed, and the tension went out of his
frame. "This is the best jam sandwich I've ever
eaten."

She flushed prettily. "It is?"

He grinned. "*Ja*, but don't tell my *mam*." He
took another bite, chewed and swallowed. "Have
you ever thought about selling this? Not the
sandwich but your strawberry jam."

"*Nay*, it never occurred to me." She grew
thoughtful. He could almost witness the work-

ings of her mind. "I could sell jams and jellies. I have a pantry filled with jars of several flavors."

"Martha's Homemade Jams and Jellies," he said, liking it. "'Tis a *gut* name for your product. And you'll need a label." He took a drink from his lemonade. "You should talk first with Bob Whittier," he said, getting into the planning stages of his idea. "He might be interested in selling them in his store."

"Hmm," she said, then ate her lunch, dropping the subject.

They enjoyed their lunch seated on the bench, side by side. Eli decided that sitting within a foot of her in the warmth of the spring sun was better than sitting across from her at the kitchen table. Here, this close to her, he could hear the soft sound of her breathing. Every time she stirred to take a bite or eat, he was aware of her every move. When a robin landed on the ground within three feet of them, he heard Martha catch her breath and then release it slowly. He watched with amazement as she pulled off a piece of sandwich, then threw it to the bird before she resumed eating.

All too soon lunch was over and it was time for Eli to get back to work. He studied the house, wondering where he should paint next, until Martha rose, capturing his attention.

"I'll carry those for you," he said as she stacked their plates and lemonade glasses.

"I can manage," she said politely, almost too politely.

He didn't react, although he was sad that she'd put up another invisible wall, as if she regretted sharing lunch with him outside. "The sandwich was delicious. I appreciate the trouble it took for you to make it."

The little frown that had settled between her eyebrows eased. "I'm glad you liked it." She bit her lip, drawing attention to her mouth. A slight breeze teased the tiny tendrils of her dark hair that had escaped from her kerchief while she was gardening earlier. She had the longest lashes, a nose that was small and rounded at the tip. He studied her mouth. Her lips were dark pink and nicely formed. He felt an odd kick to his midsection as he gazed into her brown eyes, eyes that for some reason held confusion…and maybe a little fear.

He dragged his eyes from her face to the distance, where cattle and sheep grazed in Martha's pasture. He had no business admiring Martha's features, no right to be thinking about her in any way other than as a woman who had hired him for a job.

Ike King had been dead for several months, he reminded himself, and Martha was his grieving widow. The sooner he finished this job, the better. His only focus should be on opening his own carriage shop. He stood abruptly. "I enjoyed the food. *Danki*."

Something flickered in her gaze. "You're *willkomm*."

She left for the house, and he headed back to his roller tray. Eli felt unsettled as he watched her go.

She carried the dishes to the kitchen sink and set them in the dish basin. As she washed plates and cups, Martha gazed out the window toward the bench in the backyard.

There was no sign of Eli. She went to the window and saw that his vehicle was still parked in the yard. *I shouldn't have sat outside with him.* She was inviting trouble by spending any time in his company that didn't involve a discussion or an action involving the house repairs.

She went to the sink to finish the dishes. She was overwhelmed by the urge to watch Eli work but didn't give in to it. Instead she dried the dishes and put them away before she returned to her vegetable garden.

She had knelt on a folded towel when she heard the clank of metal against wood; the noise came from the front of her house. She narrowed her gaze. *That can't be the ladder.* Intuition had her quickly setting down her spade before she stood. With brisk strides, she rounded the house, then stopped in her tracks.

"Elijah John Lapp!" she scolded when he'd taken a step up the ladder.

He froze, climbed down and faced her. He looked like a guilty little boy who'd been caught with his hand in a cookie jar.

"Have you forgotten what happened to Horseshoe Joe?" Martha regarded him sternly with her hands on her hips. She felt herself softening at his approach.

"I was just going to fix a shutter," he admitted. "It's only a few feet up."

She saw the crooked shutter in question. "Not without anyone holding your ladder." The shutter did need to be fixed as she could tell that in its present condition she wouldn't be able close or secure it against high winds and heavy rains. "Can't fixing it wait until Isaac's here?"

"Ja."

"Gut," she said firmly. "Please put the ladder away. I'd hate to see you fall and injure yourself."

He suddenly grinned, and Martha felt a sudden shift in her heart rhythm from even to rapidly unsteady. She was suddenly taken by how handsome he was, his close proximity to her and the warmth of him emanating across the distance separating them.

Her face grew hot with embarrassment.

His expression went soft. "You care about me."

She swallowed hard, shocked by his statement. "I care about all of my friends."

"Friends," he murmured. "I'm glad to know you consider me a friend."

Startled by his sudden shift in mood and the conversation, Martha could only stare at him. She frowned. "I have work to do," she said stiffly.

He appeared to be amused. "As do I."

"We ate lunch late. What time are you leaving?"

Eli raised an eyebrow. "Are you asking me to leave?"

"Nay!" Her face burned like fire. "But you shouldn't feel as if you have to stay late."

"It's only late if I think it is, and I don't," he said. He paused, his expression changing. "Maybe it is time for me to go." He seemed to watch her closely as if he'd hoped she'd encourage him to stay. She didn't. "I'll put the paint and tools into the barn."

"Put them wherever you'd like." She turned, eager to get some distance between her and this man who was having a strange effect on her. She left him for her garden to finish planting her tomato and pepper plants. Eli stayed in her thoughts as she continued to plant her seedlings. Later, after she'd realized that he must have left, she relaxed. She didn't expect him to say good-bye. He had already told her that he was leaving.

Suddenly he was there at the edge of her vege-table garden, making her gasp at his unexpected presence. The man hadn't gone after all.

"Martha."

She stood, her heart thundering in her chest. *"Ja?"*

"Do you need help?"

"Gardening?"

He nodded. "I have some time before I have to be home for supper."

"That's kind of you, Eli, but I'm finished for the day." The last thing she needed was to spend more time with Eli Lapp.

He reviewed her day's handiwork. "You should water them."

She looked at him, slightly annoyed. "I plan to." Was it all men who gave instructions with-out being asked?

"I'll help you. Do you have a watering can?" He grinned, and she realized that he'd cornered her into reluctantly accepting his help.

"I use a bucket."

He looked about as if searching for it. "Where is it?"

"In the barn." She gazed at him, surprised

by him, not for the first time. There were many facets to Elijah Lapp.

Eli headed toward the barn and was back within moments, having found the bucket easily. He filled it at the outside water pump. Then he carried it to her garden and gently poured a generous amount of water over each seedling and plant.

Martha quickly went into the house for an iced tea pitcher and filled it with water at the kitchen sink.

Despite her hope that he would go, Eli stayed, and they watered plants together, he using the bucket, she the pitcher, refilling their containers at the pump, until every seeding was thoroughly watered with a good chance for survival.

When they were done, Eli silently returned her bucket to the barn. She set the pitcher on the steps and then waited. After his help, it was the least she could do. After he came back, they walked together toward his buggy without a word.

"That was kind of you to help with my plants," she finally said. He didn't answer her at first, and she wondered what he was thinking.

"'Tis easy to be kind to you, Martha," he said quietly. Before she had a chance to react, he climbed into his vehicle and waved. "I'll see you tomorrow morning."

She watched him leave with a flutter in her chest and warmth in her heart. The man was too easy to like. She couldn't help that she did.

Friends, he'd said. *I will enjoy his friendship and that is all.*

She didn't want to think about how she'd feel one day years from now when Eli decided to court and marry one of those young girls who gravitated toward him at Sunday and church gatherings. Martha frowned. She didn't want to think about any of that now or anytime soon.

Chapter Ten

The roar of an engine followed by several rapid loud beeps woke Martha. Startled, she sprang out of bed and ran to the window on the driveway side of the house. To her shock, another large delivery truck was backing into position directly below the window. It was light outside but just barely. Had she overslept?

Windows, she thought. It was a delivery of the last windows that Samuel had ordered. She couldn't go down to sign for them. She wasn't dressed!

Panic set in as Martha debated what to do until she saw Samuel and Eli talking with the deliverymen as they unloaded the windows onto the back lawn. She watched through a crack in the white window curtains. Suddenly Eli looked up, and Martha gasped, pulled back, afraid to be seen. She still wore her nightgown and nightcap.

Did he see me? She experienced a fluttering as she hurried back into her room to dress. In less than twenty minutes, her hair was rolled, pinned and covered by her white *kapp*, and she was dressed in royal blue, ready to begin her day. She hurried downstairs to put on the coffeepot. Eli hadn't come to the door as he usually did, but the sound of the truck was loud enough to announce their presence.

As the coffee perked, Martha set about making biscuits. Then she made a double batch of sweet bread, adding chocolate chips to one loaf for Eli. She kept busy, trying not to worry whether or not Eli had seen her in the window.

Once the coffee was ready, Martha took it outside. A ladder was propped against the side of the house. Eli and Samuel stood below, deep in discussion about window replacement.

"Guder marriye!" she greeted them. *"Coffe?"*

Samuel's face brightened. *"Danki*, Martha."

She gave him a mug. Then she transferred her gaze to Eli and felt the impact of the man's watchful blue eyes.

"Smells *gut*." He accepted the cup she offered him.

"I've biscuits in the oven, and I made sweet bread with chocolate chips."

Eli gave her a slow pleased smile that made her nape tingle and her insides warm. He took a tentative sip of his coffee, his pleasure mirrored in his eyes.

"I heard the truck. I'm sorry I didn't come out to meet it," she apologized.

"It's our job to handle deliveries. I didn't expect this one so early." Samuel raised his mug to inhale the coffee's aroma. "But Eli thought we should come just in case."

She exchanged looks with Eli as his father sipped his drink. *"Danki."*

"You wouldn't have known if they were the right ones," Eli said.

"That window there—" She pointed to where she'd stood earlier. "Is that one to be replaced?"

Had they been discussing it when Eli had gestured toward where she'd stood, hidden behind the window curtain? She hoped so.

"Ja." But something in his gaze made her face heat.

"I'll check on the biscuits." She grabbed her tray and escaped. If Eli had seen her, there was nothing she could about it now. She had to get past her embarrassment and move on.

The biscuits were golden brown when she removed them from the oven. The scent of the baked goods filled the air, making her stomach rumble as she placed biscuits and slices of chocolate-chip bread on plates, which she put on the tray with butter and jam.

As she stepped outside, she saw Samuel and Eli still having a conversation about the windows. "Here you go," she said as she interrupted them to set down the tray. Their conversation looked intense, as did Eli's gaze as it settled on her. Leaving them to their work, she went quickly back to the house.

Eli stifled a small smile as he watched Martha's escape. He had seen her at the window. It was only a tiny peek, but he liked knowing that she was there, peering down at him.

"We'll do this one first," his father said.

"What time are Noah and Jedidiah coming?"

"Anytime now," *Dat* said. Eli's brothers arrived within minutes.

"I'll let Martha know we'll need to get into the upstairs rooms again," Eli offered. He knocked on her door.

"Come in, Eli," she called from inside the kitchen. "Here for coffee?" she said without turning from a cabinet where she was putting away their breakfast dishes. She faced him. "Did Isaac come? I thought I heard his voice."

Eli shook his head, enjoying the sight of her. "Jed and Noah are here." He told her of their plans for the day, then started to leave.

"Eli?"

He paused expectantly. *"Ja?"*

"Is everything all right with Isaac? I don't meant to pry, but he's not here, and Samuel seems upset." She worried her bottom lip. "I know it's none of my business—"

His expression softened at her concern. "Isaac has gone *Rumspringa*. My parents worry about him more than they did us." Eli debated whether or not to tell the rest. "He didn't come home last night."

"I'm sorry."

"Of all of us, Isaac has been the most restless."

"He is a *gut* boy," she assured him. "He will choose the Amish ways in the end."

"I hope so."

She seemed genuinely upset for him and his family. Almost as if she understood exactly how they were feeling. Eyes overly bright, she blinked them rapidly. "I'll pray that the Lord helps him to make the right decision."

"*Ja*, we all should pray for him." Eli was reluctant to leave. *"Danki."*

She looked surprised by his thanks. "For what?"

"For understanding and for believing in Isaac...and the Lord."

"We all believe in the Lord, Eli." She bit her lip. "You do believe, *ja*?"

"I've joined the church," he said, and he knew she understood his commitment to God and the

Amish faith. Men and women most often joined the church right before they married. But there were young people like him and Jedidiah who joined during their teens. They believed in the Lord, the Amish way of life and the *Ordnung* enough to make the decision to become a member of the church well before marrying. It was a big step for a young man or woman. Eli knew he'd be shunned if he ever decided to leave. He wasn't concerned, for he was happy being Amish and living the life that God intended for him. A life that would mean eventually taking a wife and having children.

"What took you so long, *soohn*?" *Dat* asked when he went back outside.

He shrugged, mumbled some excuse, then went to work.

Chapter Eleven

Martha was excited. Unable to forget Eli's suggestion of selling her jellies and jams, she drove to several shops in the area, starting with Whittier's Store and then moving on to Kitchen Kettle Village and Yoder's General Store. She spoke with the store managers to see if they would be interested in carrying her jams and jellies. Bob Whittier happily agreed. He gave her the names of other Lancaster County shops that he thought would be interested in stocking her wares, as well. Unfortunately, Bob told her, he had limited space as his was a small convenience store, but there were other larger establishments that could handle more.

Following Bob's advice, Martha drove her horse-drawn vehicle from store to store. She spoke with the owners or store managers and received a favorable response from the majority of them. But some of the managers wanted to know how many jars she could give them. Martha asked them how much they would need. She left, promising to return with a sample of her wares and the information they requested so that they would feel comfortable doing business with her. All in all, she was happy with how the day went.

As she drove home, Martha was hopeful that she'd discovered a good way to earn money. If not for Eli, she never would have given her jellies and jams another thought.

As she steered her horse toward her barnyard, Martha looked for signs of Samuel and his sons. The sky in the distance had darkened. The air held the scent of oncoming rain. There were no vehicles in the yard, so she decided that upon seeing the change in the weather, the Lapp men had finished for the day.

A heavy breeze stirred up the air as Martha got out of her vehicle. She opened the barn door and pulled both horse and buggy into the barn and shut the door. Once safely inside, she unhitched her mare from her gray buggy and put the animal in her stall.

She went to the opposite side of the structure and slid open the door. The color of the sky was now an ominous black. The storm could be seen brewing in the distance. Martha left the barn for the pasture, checking to see if the animals needed shelter. The goats were in their stalls. She brought in her milk cow. Some of the cattle had taken shelter in another outbuilding.

The sheep entered the barn with a little encouragement. Martha waited until they were in their pens before shutting the doors, secure in the knowledge that her animals were safe. She hurried back inside the barn.

A flash of lightning. A sharp crack of thunder. Martha decided to stay there until the worst of the storm blew over. A stiff breeze entered through the barn slats. The wind jostled the barn door, scaring her with the sudden noise. When the door banged against the outer walls, then started to open, she struggled against the sudden shift in the wind, a force against her as she fought to latch the doors.

The doors resisted on the pasture side. She felt a wash of cold rain spray over her face and neck as she drew them shut and was finally able to lock them into place. The animals were restless, shifting and making plaintive sounds in their stalls. Chilled by the rain that had soaked her hair, *kapp* and clothing, Martha hugged herself with her arms.

She heard a crash near the front entrance of the barn. She froze, her heart beating wildly as she realized that she wasn't alone. Someone else had sought shelter in her barn.

The storm came out of nowhere, surprising Eli as he was finishing up the far side of the farmhouse. Caught in the downpour, the only thing Eli could do was to run and seek shelter with the animals.

Martha had been gone all day. He hoped she was all right and hadn't gotten caught in the storm. He ran to the barn, slid open a door and sighed with gratitude when he slipped inside. There was a buggy inside the building. He frowned. Could it be Martha's? He didn't see or hear her come home. And then he heard her voice, and the relief that washed over him was startling to him in its intensity.

"Hallo?"

"Martha?"

"Who's there?"

"It's me. Eli Lapp." He hurried toward her voice, saw her huddled against the wall on the opposite end of the barn. She had turned on a battery-operated lantern. He could see her face silhouetted in the golden glow, saw the way she flinched with every lightning flash and clap of thunder. Lightning illuminated the interior of the barn through the hayloft window, brief flashes that came in a series, followed by rumbling thunder or loud cracks.

"Eli!" She saw him as he maneuvered around Ike's farm equipment. She seemed glad to see him. He was relieved that she was okay as he approached. Dampness made her hair and garments cling. Her head covering was askew, probably caught and shifted by the wind. Raindrops splattered her dress. He'd never been happier that she was here safe beside him.

"I couldn't close the door," she admitted with a wry smile.

"The wind out there is fierce." He felt the impact of being alone with her. "Not to worry— your new windows are shut tight and locked."

"What are you still doing here?" she asked.

"*Dat* left me to work awhile longer. I was going to walk to Jacob's and ask him for a ride home."

"I'll take you home after the storm passes." She winced at the loud boom of thunder that continued to rumble on for several seconds.

"Where did you go today?" Eli was curious.

"I took your advice and spoke with several local store owners about stocking my jams and jellies. Many of them were receptive."

He smiled, pleased for her. "That's wonderful." A flash of lightning drew his gaze up to the hayloft window.

"I plan to go out again in the next day or two and bring samples."

They chatted about her venture until a sudden silence descended, broken only by the sound of the rain on the barn roof. Eli shifted closer, overly aware of the sound made by Martha's breathing, the scent of her homemade scented soap...and the way she shifted and moved as she stood next to him. He studied her features, liking what he saw. Long lashes surrounded eyes a beautiful shade of brown. Her nose was perfectly formed, her lips pink, but he wouldn't dare think about trying to kiss her.

Martha shifted uncomfortably, and Eli realized that he was staring. "Finished up the house. That's why I stayed late. We completed installing the last of the windows, the shutters and the two doors. All that's left is to caulk a few roof shingles."

She frowned. "You're going up onto my roof?"

Eli shrugged. "Better me than Isaac or *Dat*." There was a heightened sense of awareness between them in the darkened interior of the barn.

He watched and listened as Martha easily calmed the livestock with soft words and a gentle touch. The air held the scent of farm animals, offensive to some perhaps but not to him. Animal smells were part of daily farm life, and he'd lived on a farm since he was born.

A cow mooed, then quieted as Martha murmured to her and rubbed the bovine's side. The sheep baaed in their pen, and her two goats bleated before they settled down in their stalls.

The rain fell harder. It thundered against the roof as the wind increased, buffeting the sides of the barn. Eli followed Martha to watch how she calmed and managed the animals. She turned, and they nearly collided. Eli instinctively reached out to steady her. They stared at each other a long moment before Martha looked away and put some distance between them.

Eli followed her, unable to keep away. He wanted desperately to spend time with Martha. But a little voice inside warned him that he shouldn't be alone with her. He stopped and watched her without taking another step.

Martha went from stall to stall, speaking soothingly to her animals. Her voice calmed them, and he understood why. He felt pleased and calmed by her sweet voice, too.

"They should be fine now," she said with a smile.

He nodded, struck again by how much in her element she seemed. A long silence ensued, filled with only the raging storm outside, which was starting to move away. The sounds faded into the distant sky.

Dampness filled the air with scents and moisture. Martha shifted on her feet and made a move toward the barn door as if to check outside.

He followed her. "'Tis far from over," he said, coming up from behind. "You may want to wait awhile."

Startled by his voice, she turned. He saw something flicker on her face, and he stepped away to give her room. The barn was filled with animals and farm equipment—and Martha's gray buggy. He and Martha were left with a small area of the barn to wait out the bad weather.

"Martha," he began, unsure of what he wanted to say. She looked at him with confusion.

And then they heard the sound...a *ping, ping, ping.* He felt a splash of water on his face. He looked up, saw the roof leaking and sighed. "Add 'patch one leaking roof' to my list," he said jokingly.

She glanced up and frowned.

"Bucket in the same place?" he asked.

"*Ja.* In the front of the barn near my buggy."

He quickly went for the bucket before she had a chance to move. He returned to place it on the floor under the leak. "Do you have another one?" Water dripped from above, splashing on Martha's and Eli's upturned faces.

She looked thoughtful. "I have a large stainless bowl that I use for canning vegetables. It's up front."

He raised his eyebrows. "Where?"

"On a shelf near the door. It's too big for a kitchen cabinet."

"Wait here. I'll get it." He started to leave.

"Eli." Her call stopped him in his strides.

He turned and waited. She held up a small flashlight, clicked it on. "You may need this."

He nodded, pleased when she met him halfway. He could use the flashlight; it had gotten dark in the barn. He took the battery lamp, aware of the heat left by her fingers on its metal base. Attraction sizzled between them.

He knew he was in trouble. If he were smart, he'd get out of the barn and away from Martha as quickly as he could run.

But he didn't want to leave. *Nay.* He was starting to like Ike King's widow more than he should, and there was nothing he could do about it but pray for the feeling to pass.

Martha stood in the golden glow of her lantern and watched as Eli left to fetch her canning bowl. She heard the sound of water striking against metal. She groaned. Rain was coming through the roof and hitting Ike's new farm equipment.

The rain hammered in a steady roar against

the barn. Alone, Martha felt the intensity of the storm more so than when Eli Lapp stood by her side. She was glad that he was near. The thought of being alone during the storm was unnerving. And while his appearance had frightened her at first, she had quickly become relieved once she knew the intruder wasn't an intruder at all.

Her cow mooed, and Martha stepped into its stall to soothe her. Eli came back as she left the cow and returned to where she'd waited.

He held up a large stainless steel bowl. "This it?"

"*Ja*, that should catch the water for a while."

Ping. Ping. Ping. They exchanged looks. "Another leak," she said.

"I'll take a look." He headed toward the sound, disappearing from sight as a bright flash of lightning lit up the barn, seeping in through every tiny crack in the barn siding. The ensuing thunder was loud and startling even though Martha expected it. "Eli?"

"Coming!"

She knew immediate relief when she saw the light from his flashlight beaming across the barn floor. He appeared just when she felt like she could no longer stand to be alone. Her heart picked up its pace when he loomed ahead and grinned at her. The effect he had on her whenever he was near worried her.

Ping ping ping! He gave her wry smile as he shook his head. "It's the bowl, not the equipment. I found your canning pot and used that, too."

"'Tis *gut* that you're here," she admitted, and he looked delighted. "I don't like being alone during thunderstorms."

His expression changed. "'Tis frightening, isn't it?"

She nodded, but she no longer was afraid now that he was here. She wondered what it would be like to be young and have someone like Eli Lapp in love with her. Would he make a *gut* husband? She already suspected by his obvious affection for his nephew that he would make a good father.

Her rampant thoughts made her feel slightly ill. She liked Eli Lapp; of course she did. He was a kind man who had helped her on more than one occasion. But these thoughts she was having of him were wrong. She didn't want another man in her life. And even if she did—which she didn't—Eli Lapp was too young and too much of a charmer for her. When he was eventually ready to settle down, he could have his pick of the girls in their Amish community. Still, just because he wasn't right for her—and she didn't want to be hurt by another man—didn't mean that she couldn't appreciate a good-looking man.

Horrified by her continuing thoughts about how attractive Eli was, she moved away toward the far wall, where she hugged herself with her arms. There was a wooden bench that Ike had used as a small workbench, and she sat down on it. If he thought it strange that she didn't say a word, Eli didn't let on. He simply followed her and sat beside her. She felt his presence in his scent, the warmth of him sitting close. Tears stung her eyes, and she blinked them away. Even if things had been different, there was little chance of winning such a man's heart...and there was every chance that she couldn't give him, or any man, a child.

"Martha." His voice startled her. "Are you all right?"

She nodded silently even though inside it felt as if her heart were breaking in two. "I'm fine." At least, she was trying to be fine.

He didn't comment. There was a long silent moment during which she could feel his intense regard. She refused to meet his gaze. "The storm is moving away," he finally said. "Before we leave for *gut*, we'll make sure this roof is fixed. I don't want you to worry about your animals or equipment."

She faced him. His lips curved upward in a slow smile that made her heart slam into her chest. When he looked at her that way, she could barely formulate a coherent thought.

He furrowed his brown. "Martha?"

"Ja?" She felt the stark sensation of their locked gazes.

"Listen," Eli whispered. "The rain stopped." He stood, and she followed suit, trailing him as he opened the barn door. They were greeted by bright sunlight and a landscape awash in wet glorious colors of vivid greens and the yellow, red and pink blossoms planted near the house.

"Look!" She pointed toward the sky, enthralled with the prettiest rainbow that she'd ever seen. Entranced, she stepped out of the barn and stared up at the sky streaked with a myriad of color and light. "'Tis beautiful," she gasped.

"Ja," he said into her ear. She turned and smiled, and her lips froze as she realized that he'd been staring at her, not the rainbow. Martha caught her breath, unable to turn away. Her heart pumped hard to bring in oxygen.

The moment of startling awareness passed. "I should get home," he said crisply.

"I'll take you."

"I can walk to Jacob's."

Determined, Martha moved to block his way until he was forced to acknowledge her stubborn streak. "I'll take you. 'Tis the least I do."

He gave an abrupt nod. *"Oll recht."* He skirted the outside of the barn toward the other barn door and the buggy inside.

"Eli."

"Ja?" He seemed to stiffen as if reluctant to stop and turn around, but he did.

"Danki for waiting out the storm with me." She smiled warmly, hoping to put him at ease. Those tense moments in the barn had been unsettling to them both, she realized.

She must have been convincing, because he seemed to relax. "We couldn't risk getting wet, could we?" he teased, looking more like the Eli she'd first gotten to know.

He threw open the other barn door, and the two of them managed to back the horse and buggy out of the building. Soon they were riding toward the Lapp farm with Eli at the leathers. She didn't want to make a big deal out of his driving when the vehicle belonged to her. Besides, it was nice to be driven by a man again.

She was conscious of Eli beside her on the seat. She couldn't help notice the way his strong hands easily controlled the reins and how his masculine frame filled his half of the front seat. She detected the scent of dampness, outdoors and a pleasant smell that could only belong to him.

With a silent groan, Martha faced the side window and closed her eyes. *What am I doing? Thinking such things again?* She was a foolish, lonely widow, but she wouldn't give in. She had a life to live, and she would live it within the Amish faith on her own terms.

"We're here," Eli announced unnecessarily as he pulled onto the road to his father's farm.

Martha was quiet as he drew the buggy to a stop not far from the house. "That didn't take too long," she said with a smile.

"Nay," he agreed with a disconcerting intensity.

"Do I have a speck on my nose?" she asked, curious.

"Something," he murmured, and the air between them suddenly filled with tension. The door to the farmhouse opened, and several Lapps spilled out of the house and raced in their direction. The mood was gone so quickly she thought that she might have imagined it. *Thank the Lord.*

"Eli!" Katie Lapp exclaimed as she approached. "We were concerned about you."

He climbed out of the vehicle. "I'm fine, *Mam.*" He smiled to reassure her. "I took shelter from the storm in Martha's barn."

Katie looked from one to the other silently and then said, "I see." She smiled at Martha. "Will you come in for tea?"

"I appreciate the invitation, Katie, but I should get home."

The woman nodded as if she understood. "Come and visit soon," Katie said as Martha slid into position on the seat behind the leathers. "Into the house," Eli's mother urged her curious children. Everyone left, leaving Eli and Martha alone.

"It was *gut* of you to help with the roof leaks," she said.

"I was happy to help." He glanced toward the house, and it was as if a shutter had closed off his expression when he looked back. "You will be all right going home?"

"*Ja*. I know how to drive my buggy. I've done it many times." She grinned to let him know that she was poking fun. She heard him draw a sharp breath, watched as he shook his head. A reluctant grin curved up the lines of his beautiful male mouth.

"I will see you soon, Martha. Appreciate the ride."

"Have a *gut* night, Elijah Lapp," she said formally. With a gentle flick of the leathers, she expertly turned the buggy toward home.

Minutes later, as she pulled her vehicle onto the main road, Martha glanced back toward the Samuel Lapp farmhouse. She was startled to see Eli standing where she'd left him. The knowledge caused a fluttering in her belly. Then just as quickly fear rose, forcing the pleasant feeling away. No matter how much she might have wished it, she wasn't the right woman for Eli

Lapp or any man. After he finished the last of the repairs, she'd have to do everything she could to avoid him without seeming rude. It was the only way to get over her foolish, girlish thoughts.

Chapter Twelve

After watching Martha's departure, Eli headed toward the house. His mother stood on the porch waiting for him. "Nice of Martha to bring you home," she said with a small smile.

He nodded and then narrowed his gaze. There was a look in his mother's eyes that alarmed him. "*Mam*, what's wrong? 'Tis Isaac, isn't it? He's not hurt, is he?"

She shook her head, but Eli could see that Isaac was the one causing her concern. "*Nay.* Your *bruder* is home, but he's not talking. Your *dat* tried to speak with him, and so did I. But he gives only single-word answers. We have no idea where he's been or who he was with."

Eli settled a hand on his mother's shoulder. "I'll talk with him. He'll answer me." He'd make sure of it.

"I hope so." *Mam* hugged herself with her arms. "He's in your room."

He hated when his mother worried. Entering the house, he headed directly to the upstairs bedroom he and Isaac had shared since Jacob had married and moved into his own place.

Eli entered to find Isaac sitting on his bed, staring out the window. He studied his younger brother for a long moment. "Isaac."

His brother turned, saw Eli standing just his doorway and scowled. "What are you doing here?"

"Why are you so defensive? You're on *Rumspringa, ja*? Do you think I've come to scold you?" Eli sat on his bed and smiled. He would have to tread lightly if he was ever to learn where Isaac had been last night or why his brother seemed reluctant to confess what he'd been doing.

"*Mam* and *Dat* were worried about you," Eli said softly.

Emotion worked in Isaac's expression. He appeared remorseful. "I didn't mean to worry them."

"They don't mind if you go out and explore the English world, Isaac. But when you didn't let them know that you'd be gone overnight, they became frightened. They love you. The English world can be harsh. They feared that something bad happened to you."

His brother blinked back tears. "I'm sorry."

Eli smiled, sensing that his brother was more than ready to talk. "In the future, remember to let someone know if you're spending the night elsewhere. *Ja?*" He stood and moved to the door.

"Eli."

Eli halted. *"Ja?"*

"May I confide in you?" Isaac looked nervous yet clearly excited for some reason.

"Anytime," Eli assured him.

"Now?"

Eli nodded. He returned to sit on his bed and sat facing his younger brother. "What is it?"

Isaac's expression changed. His eyes filled with pleasure as if he was extraordinarily pleased about what he was about to confess. "I met a girl."

"Ah, a girl." Eli grinned. "Who is she?"

"Her name is Nancy," Isaac said.

"Nancy," Eli echoed. He tried to recall a young woman named Nancy close to Isaac's age in their church district, but he couldn't think of one. There was Nancy King, Amos and Mae's youngest daughter, but she had married and was happy with their sister-in-law's brother Josiah. "Have I met her?"

"*Nay*. I doubt if you're even seen her," Isaac said. "Her name is Nancy Smith."

"From which church district?" Eli furrowed his brow. "I'm not familiar with any Amish Smiths, but then I don't know about the church districts west of Lancaster city." He saw a shutter came down over Isaac's expression, and Eli knew. "She's English."

"*Ja*." His brother seemed pleased that he'd guessed correctly.

"And you like her," Eli said, watching his brother's reaction closely. "A lot." He sighed. Their mother and father wouldn't be happy. "Where did you meet?"

"At the movie theater."

"You went to the movies?" Eli raised his eyebrows. "Bet that was fun."

"*Ja*." Isaac, who had immediately seemed defensive again, brightened.

"What did you see?" Eli inhaled silently, focusing to say calm.

Isaac appeared embarrassed. *"Frozen."*

"What is frozen?" Then he remembered the items that were everywhere in the big-box stores, plastered with colorful drawings of two girls— one with white hair and one with red. "You watched an animated film."

"*Ja*, with singing and music. The movie was released a while ago," he explained. "It was a special showing." He warmed to the telling of his evening out. "We—Henry Miller and I— were walking along Newport Road when we met up with Nancy and her friend Jessica. They were shopping, but they hadn't bought anything. They said that they wanted to buy pretzels, and I told them the best place to find them. Then they asked us if we wanted to go to the movies with them. We said yes. I never saw a movie before... and I was curious."

"How did you get there?" Eli asked quietly.

"Jessica has a car."

Eli wondered how old Jessica was. "I see."

"I can't be punished for seeing a movie during *Rumspringa, ja?*"

He nodded. It was true that *Rumspringa,* which meant running around, was the time in a young person's life before joining the church where he or she was allowed to experience the world outside their Amish community. The idea was to allow them this freedom so that they could make an informed decision about whether or not they wanted to join the Amish church or leave their community for a different life. Most children of Amish parents chose to join the church as he, Jacob and his older brothers had.

Eli understood why *Mam* and *Dat* were concerned about Isaac. His brother seemed to be constantly searching in his life for something more. His parents feared that Isaac would be the one to get into trouble with English teenagers. And what if Isaac decided not to join the Amish faith but to leave? *Mam* and *Dat* would accept his decision because they would have to, but they would be heartbroken with him gone.

"You've done nothing wrong in seeing a movie, Isaac," Eli explained, "but you chose badly when you didn't tell *Mam* and *Dat* that you'd be staying out all night." He sighed. He felt somewhat sorry for his young misguided brother. "The deed is done. You should apologize to them." With a smile, he placed a hand on Isaac's arm. "Tell me about Nancy Smith."

Isaac's features brightened as he began to describe Nancy's smile, her pretty face and her obvious interest in him. How they'd sat together in the movie theater and she'd reached for his hand, how he'd never felt this way about a girl before.

"After the movie, we went for pizza and then I walked her home. We sat on her front steps and talked for hours. Then I left and met up again with Henry. He'd been talking with Jessica. It was late, and I didn't want to disturb everyone at home, so I stayed at Henry's. We promised to meet up with the girls for an early breakfast tomorrow morning. It had to be early because Nancy and Jessica are still in school." His brother grinned.

Isaac and Henry were finished with school. Within their Amish community, children attended school through the eighth grade. "Are you planning to see her again?" Eli asked.

Isaac's eyes gleamed, and a soft smile altered his features. "For an early breakfast tomorrow, then again on Friday. The girls have a short school day. We told them we'd meet them at the Rockvale Outlets."

Eli gaped at him. "You and Henry are going shopping?"

Isaac narrowed his eyes. "You don't approve."

"*Nay*, I don't approve or disapprove. I'm just surprised. I didn't think you would like to shop. And the Rockvale Outlets are not close. How do you plan to get there?"

"Henry says we can hire Jeff Martin to drive us."

Eli nodded in understanding. Jeff was Rick Martin's son. Rick and his family were good neighbors and friends. Rick had been extremely helpful after Horseshoe Joe's accident when he'd fallen off a ladder and had to be rushed to the hospital. Rick had driven Annie and her brother numerous times to the hospital, and he'd taken Joe to his doctor's appointments after Joe had come home to recuperate.

"Is Jeff a *gut* driver?"

Isaac inclined his head. "Henry says so. He's ridden with him before."

"And Henry is going tomorrow, too?"

"*Ja*. He likes Jessica, maybe not as much as I like Nancy, but he doesn't mind going."

"You need to tell *Dat* and *Mam* of your plans." Eli's lips firmed. "After you apologize to them."

Isaac blanched. "Both of them?"

"*Ja*." Eli rose. "And as soon as possible. They love you. Remember that."

"I will talk with them," Isaac promised in a voice almost too low to hear.

Smiling, Eli left the room and went downstairs, where he met his mother in the kitchen. *Mam* had cut some basil and parsley from the plants flourishing in her greenhouse. She had washed them and now was setting them out to dry.

"Isaac is ready to talk with you and *Dat*," he told her.

Katie looked relieved as she reached behind to retie her apron strings. "Will we like what he has to say?"

"Probably not. But he'll be more open about what he does if he believes you won't judge or scold him."

"There are consequences after a wrongdoing," *Mam* said with a frown. "I can't promise there won't be."

"Fair enough."

They heard Isaac's footsteps on the stairs. "I'm going to check on the animals," Eli said while his mother moved to stand near the kitchen sink and wait for Isaac to appear.

He heard Isaac's voice as he closed the outside door behind him. "*Mam*, can I talk with you and *Dat*?"

His mother's response reached him before he was out of hearing range. "You can talk with us anytime, *soohn*," she said.

As he entered the barn, Eli's thoughts turned to the recent thunderstorm and the woman who had sought shelter with him in her barn. *Martha*. He felt a rush of pleasure. The widow was special. He had no right to like her so much. He still had to contend with opening his carriage shop. Until his business was a reality and a viable concern, he had only a vision of hope for the future.

His attraction toward the woman disturbed him greatly. He knew there was repair work to finish at Martha's farm, but he wasn't ready to see her again. Which was probably ridiculous since finishing up would ensure that he wouldn't have to see her each day and contend with his growing feelings. So he would refocus on his future business. Figure out exactly what he needed to set up shop. He would start by visiting other carriage shops in Lancaster County. He needed to know how to begin. He had more than twenty thousand dollars saved—that was good start-up money. Until Lapp's Buggy Shop was open and earning money, there would be no woman in his life.

"Eli." His father entered the barn minutes after Eli was done feeding the horses and checking on the goats. "Your *mudder* and I talked with Isaac. Your *bruder* has apologized and told us of his plans."

"He didn't mean to hurt you," Eli said with a small smile. "He wasn't thinking."

"Not of us, his family."

"Dat?" he asked, changing the subject. "How much do you think it will take for me to open my carriage shop?"

His father gave it some thought. "You should talk with Noah. He can help you better than I."

"I'm just wondering how many more years I'll have to work before I have saved enough money." He rubbed a hand across his brow. "I thought I'd visit other carriage businesses, see what I can learn."

"That's a fine idea."

Eli nodded. "Do you mind if I take the day tomorrow?"

"Ja, go."

"Who will work at Martha's tomorrow?"

"We are almost done there. It can wait."

"What about sending Isaac to finish up?"

"*Nay*. He will be having breakfast with a girl."

Eli felt relieved that his brother had told their parents about Nancy. "Isaac told you about her— about Nancy."

His *dat* frowned. "Nancy?"

"The girl he likes. The one he'll be meeting for breakfast." Eli frowned. "He didn't tell you that he's seeing an *Englisher*?"

Dat released a sharp breath. "*Nay*, he didn't."

"Give him time. Isaac will tell you about her when he's ready."

His father agreed. "Sooner than later, I hope. He plans to bring someone to the house for supper next week."

Eli grinned. "He's not hiding her. His feelings for this girl are new and scary for him." *Like mine*, he thought with the stark realization of the truth. "May I take the wagon?" A simple horse-drawn four-wheeled vehicle was exactly what he needed to enjoy the extended ride and the day.

"That's fine," his *dat* said. "We won't be needing it."

Eli sighed with relief. He might feel something for Martha King, but a day away from the widow would put things into proper prospective. He would figure out what he needed to do next for his carriage business and proceed from there.

Chapter Thirteen

Martha tossed and turned most of the night, falling asleep at dawn only to awake again two hours later. She couldn't stop thinking about Eli. During their time together in the barn, she'd been aware of him as never before. *I have strong feelings for him*, she thought, frowning. She would forget him. She didn't want to make the same mistake as before. He was a young man with plans that didn't include a widow who had no intention of ever getting married again. She sat up in bed and shook her head. To spend any amount of time with him would be foolish.

She was in the kitchen brewing coffee when she heard a wagon roll into the yard. She pulled out two coffee mugs and set them on the counter. Then adjusting her *kapp* to set it straight, she went to greet the workers. She was surprised to find her sister-in-law, Mae.

"Martha, *guder marriye!*"

"*Guder marriye*, Mae! I didn't expect to see you this morning, but I'm glad you came." She smiled as she gestured Mae inside. *"Coffe?"*

"I can't stay. I'm heading into town, and I promised Samuel I'd stop here on my way." She stepped from her buggy. "The Lapp boys won't be coming today."

Martha was concerned. "Did something happen?"

"*Nay.* Everyone is fine but busy. The only one who could've come is Eli and he has errands to run today. He'll return to finish up tomorrow."

She felt relieved. "I appreciate you letting me know."

"The *haus* is looking wonderful. Samuel and his *soohns* do wonderful work."

"*Ja*, they do." She was more than pleased with their skilled handiwork.

Mae gestured toward the barn. "Samuel said the roof leaks."

The memory of her and Eli's time in the barn made warmth flood Martha's face. She hoped that Mae didn't notice because she wasn't ready to explain. Fortunately, Mae was eyeing the barn and not her.

"*Ja*, in several places. Eli said that he would fix it."

"*Gut, gut,*" Mae said as she met Martha's gaze

with a smile. "I'd best go. Amos will be wanting an early lunch, and I need to get my shopping in before I head home."

"*Danki* for stopping by, Mae."

"'Tis always a pleasure to see you, Martha," Mae said warmly. She seemed to hesitate. "You're managing fine on your own?"

"I'm doing well," she said, meaning it. "'Tis different with him gone. I find that my time is my own." She smiled to reassure her. "I'm content." Or she would be if she didn't have a strange awareness of Elijah Lapp, she thought.

Mae seemed to accept what she was saying. "To enjoy one's own time. To me, that sounds like a blessing from the Lord."

Martha reached up to brush a bug away from her face. "That's how I choose to see it."

Mae left shortly afterward, and Martha went back into the house. As she puttered about her kitchen, washing up plates and coffee mugs from that morning, then assembling jars of jelly and jam samples to bring to local merchants, she thought of the busy day ahead. If all went well, by this time next month she'd have earned income from her jelly sales with more to follow. The other day she'd noticed an Eggs for Sale sign on the side of the road. She had some good laying chickens. Why couldn't she sell eggs, too?

She laughed out loud with joy. This would

be a busy summer, making jellies and jams and collecting eggs to sell. These were good ways to earn money. Maybe she'd think of more. And it was all because of Eli Lapp.

Eli continually thought of Martha as he milled about the carriage shops he visited. He'd been mistaken to believe that staying away from her farm would put things in better perspective. She was still uppermost in his mind.

He'd overreacted in the barn. The storm, the darkness, the close proximity of him and Martha as lightning flashed and thunder crashed overhead had been a bit overwhelming, and he'd panicked.

Things would be different when he saw her again. He would feel comfortable around her, more relaxed. He would tell her how he felt, and she would smile, tell him that she liked him, too.

As he headed for home, Eli found himself looking forward to seeing her again, of getting back to finish the last of her repairs. Once he completed the work, he could put his attraction to Martha aside and focus on his carriage-making business. Today he'd realized with excitement that he had enough money to rent shop space and buy his initial supplies. He was looking to serve his small community; he was not aiming to open a huge business with several em-

ployees and a customer base of both Amish and
English. Not that he wouldn't help anyone who
came into his shop. But he wanted to keep it simple and small. He was a craftsman with experience from helping friends and neighbors. When
he was a teenager, he'd learned a lot about the
craft when he'd worked in a carriage shop just
outside of Bird in Hand.

He thought of his brother Noah, who owned
and operated his successful furniture business.
Dat had suggested that he should talk with
Noah, and that was what he planned to do next.
His brother would know the best location. He
had to pass Noah's on his way home. Would his
brother be at work or at home? *Only one way to
find out.*

It was midafternoon when Eli parked his two-
wheeled buggy in the parking lot next to Noah's
furniture business. He tied Janey to the hitching
post and then took off his hat before he entered
through the front door. "Noah! You here?"

Noah came out of the back room, brightening when he saw Eli. "I wouldn't be leaving the
door open if I wasn't," he teased. He glanced
down Eli's length, noting his choice of clothes.

"You weren't at Martha's?" He looked
thoughtful. "Isaac said you were checking out
your future competition."

"I've been visiting carriage businesses today,

figuring what I'd need." He hung his hat on the back of a beautifully crafted chair. "I don't think of them as my competition. I don't want a shop that big."

Noah nodded as if he understood. "You're ready to look for a place."

"With your help."

Looking pleased, his brother gestured for Eli to sit in a chair. "How can I help you?"

"How did you know where to open your shop? I have no idea where to look first."

"Your goal is to service our Happiness Amish community, *ja*?"

"*Ja*. Most of the other carriage makers have a large English customer base. I will certainly help any of our English neighbors, but I want to focus on working for our community."

"You don't want a place like Mitch's," Noah said.

Eli nodded. He had worked for a time at a carriage shop run by Mitch Logan, an *Englisher* who sold new tackle and carriages to mostly English clientele. Eli had applied for a job there when he was younger after hearing that Mitch was looking for someone to do buggy repairs. Eli had worked on his family's vehicles as well as their neighbors' and friends'. He'd known how to change a wheel and replace a part on or mend a carriage body. That one summer he'd worked at Mitch's before his father had needed him on the farm for the fall harvest.

"I thought I'd need a lot more money, but I realized differently. I want to work to open it soon. The longer I put this off, the higher the start-up cost will be." He told Noah the amount of his savings.

Noah's eyes widened. "You've saved over twenty thousand dollars?" Eli nodded. "I think you're right. It's the right time to look for a location." His brother looked delighted. "You should have more than enough to open up your small shop. Your customers will supply the rest."

Eli had hoped that Noah would say that. "So what do you think? Have any thoughts where?"

"I think I have an idea," Noah said mysteriously, "but I'll need a few days before I can tell you." He paused. "In case it doesn't work out." He headed into the back workroom with Eli following. "No sense raising up your hopes only to have them dashed."

He had the time. He'd waited this long. Why not a couple more days? Besides, there was still the work to finish up at Martha's. "Appreciate it."

He widened his eyes as he saw what his brother was working on. "Is that what I think it is?"

"*Ja*, a cradle." Noah smiled. The furniture was a simple piece that was well crafted and beautifully finished. "I just put on a second coast of varnish."

Eli examined the cradle closely, curious about the customer who'd commissioned the work. "Who's it for?"

"Rachel." Noah beamed. "I was afraid to make one for Katy."

"You and Rachel?" He saw his brother's joy and felt happy for him. And he understood Noah's fears. Rachel had miscarried their first child.

"*Ja*. We never thought…"

"Katy is still a baby."

Noah nodded. "I can't say that I'm not worried. But the Lord blessed us with a beautiful, healthy daughter, and I've been praying that He's decided to bless us with another child."

"Do *Mam* and *Dat* know?"

Noah shook his head. "*Nay*, and please don't tell them. You're the first I've told, and I have to ask you not to say a word to anyone."

"Not a word," Eli promised.

Noah looked pleased. *"Danki."*

"Let me know if there is anything I can do to help." He gazed at the cradle. It was beautiful. One day he hoped to have a cradle like this one with a child of his own sleeping inside. And it was Martha he envisioned holding his baby. "I can deliver this one for you," he offered with a grin.

Noah laughed. "*Nay, bruder.* This delivery is mine to make."

Chapter Fourteen

As he drove to the King farm the next morning, Eli was alone. Despite his misgivings regarding her, he looked forward to seeing Martha again. Why should he worry about spending time with her when it looked as if he was close to finally opening his business? Perhaps the strange tension in the air between him and Martha during the storm was due to the intensity of the lightning and the thunder. Anyone would have been affected by the bad storm.

It was a beautiful morning that promised to be warm. The birds had been chirping merrily when he'd gotten up that morning, and upon exiting the house, he had detected the scent of the roses and honeysuckle that his mother had planted by the front porch.

Today, *Dat* and his younger brothers had farmwork to do. His mother and Hannah were in *Mam*'s greenhouse, checking on the herbs and vegetable plants *Mam* had planted from seeds before the onset of spring. Katie Lapp, noted for her garden plants, often gave them away to family and friends. Occasionally she earned a little money when she sold them to the English.

Earlier in the week, he had seen Martha working in her vegetable garden. Would she be gardening today?

Martha King's farm loomed into view ahead. Eli slowed his horse, then steered Randy, their gelding, onto the dirt driveway. There was no sign of the widow in the yard when he pulled up near the barn and parked the buggy. With a tentative smile on his face, he stepped down from his vehicle and crossed the yard to knock on her back door. As he had in the past, he didn't wait for an answer before he opened the door and stepped inside, shutting it behind him. And then he saw her at the stove. He couldn't see what she was cooking, but it didn't matter. The sight of her nearly stole his breath. "Martha."

"Eli!" she gasped. She spun to face him and cried out as her hand caught the side of a hot cast-iron skillet.

"Ach!" He rushed to her side to immediately turn on the faucet. He let the water run while he gently captured her hand and carefully examined her burn. "I frightened you," he said hus-

kily. "I'm sorry. I thought you heard me close the door."

"'Tis not your fault. I was woolgathering and didn't hear you come in," she said as Eli gently moved her burned hand under the faucet. She winced as the cold water hit her damaged skin. She withdrew her hand within seconds, and he frowned at her red and blistered skin.

"Where can I get ice?" he asked. He felt terrible for causing her injury. The last thing he wanted to do was to hurt her.

"Back room." She put her hand into the running water again, then jerked it back, wincing again as she studied the burned flesh.

Eli turned off the faucet and placed the tea towel that was lying on the counter along the edge of the sink and under her dripping fingers. Then he hurried to get ice from the freezer in the back room. He popped two ice cubes out of the tray, his fingers instantly feeling the chill, and returned to gently take her hand. He took hold of her wrist with one hand, and with the thumb of his other against her palm, he pressed the ice lightly against her wound. The ice melted and dripped and he hoped brought her some relief. "Maybe we should hold it over the sink." He studied the burn wound with growing concern before he shifted her hand so that the water dripped into the sink rather than on the dish towel. He firmed his lips as he gazed at her. She didn't look well, and he'd prefer it if she could sit down. "Do you have any burn salve?"

Martha nodded. "'Tis not my first burn." Her crooked smile affected him deeply.

Eli studied her pale features. He didn't like the knowledge that she'd suffered burns in the past when he hadn't been here to help her. *But Ike was.* He didn't like being reminded that Martha was still a grieving widow. He wanted things to be different. He wanted them to be friends. *Perhaps more than friends.* "Where is it?" he asked, referring to the salve.

"In the top cabinet near the stove."

"Makes sense." He smiled at her warmly. "Hold this in place." He watched as she used her opposite hand to keep the ice on her burn. Satisfied, he went to the cabinet and retrieved the burn ointment. He recalled when Jacob had suffered a nasty burn when he first started working at the forge. The wound had been extremely painful, and he had felt sorry for his brother. He couldn't recall a time when he'd gotten burned, but, according to his mother, apparently he had when as a five-year-old child he'd reached for a cupcake from a hot tin *Mam* had taken out of the oven.

He closed his fingers over the melting ice, taking over for Martha, who seemed grateful for his help. They locked gazes, and he smiled again to reassure her. Then he removed the ice and dabbed carefully at the burn with a paper towel before he gingerly spread the ointment over her wounded skin.

"I think we should cover the burn with a bandage," he said. Fortunately, he thought her wound small enough that a couple of bandages would do.

"Oll recht." Using her good hand, she opened the closest cabinet door, where she took out a box of fabric bandages before she handed them to him.

Eli unwrapped the bandage and placed it over her burn with gentle fingers. After setting another one beside it to ensure the wound was fully covered, he looked up to gauge the depth of her pain. There were tiny furrows on her forehead as she eyed his handiwork. When he experienced the strongest desire to draw her into his arms to comfort her, he was startled, even shocked, at the depth of his feelings. "I'm sorry."

She gave him a weak smile. "I was thinking of other things, Eli. This wasn't your fault."

"But if I hadn't startled you..."

"I heard a knock and vaguely remember the door closing. I simply didn't react like I should have, especially with an unlocked door."

"Is there anything else I can do?" He wanted to stay and spend the day with her, but wouldn't… couldn't.

"Your *dat* and *bruders*…?"

"Didn't come with me this morning. I should be able to finish the remainder of the repairs without them. *Dat* and Isaac might stop by, but I doubt it." He felt his gaze drawn to her features—her smooth skin, her bright brown eyes… her upturned nose…her full pink lips. There was warmth in her expression despite the pain of her burn. A tiny smile played about her lips and entered her gaze, but then it faded. Eli realized that he must have frightened her with the intensity of his concern for her.

He felt his heart slam into his throat and wondered if she could hear it.

She looked away as if suddenly nervous. *Why?* Had she guessed that he was struggling with newfound feelings for her? Was she uncomfortable with the knowledge? With his presence? The thought made his chest burn.

"Better?" he asked, hoping that she was. He was relieved to see her nod. He attempted to lighten the mood. "What's in the pan?" He bent closer to look. "Were you making sweet corn bread?"

She regarded him with sudden amusement.

"Ja." She flexed her hand and winced. "Would you like to try some?"

He wanted to prolong his time with her but knew it was wise to go. *"Nay.* Perhaps later? Before I leave? I should get to work now."

She'd be hurting for a while, he thought, but eventually the burn should heal and the mark would disappear. Eli sniffed the corn bread and closed his eyes at the delicious aroma. "Save me a piece for later?"

"Nay," she teased. "I plan to eat the entire pan myself."

He grinned, delighted with her teasing, while his heart seemed to skitter and dance inside his chest. He murmured something about seeing her later before he left the house and headed toward the barn. He was breathing rapidly as he crossed the yard. He stifled the urge to look back. Would he see her in the window?

Despite spending the day away from her to refocus on his future carriage shop, he'd known that there would be no escaping his growing feelings for Martha King. But he doubted she felt the same. First, there was the fact that Ike had died only last autumn, and then there was the seven years difference in their ages. A difference that didn't bother him, but he knew instinctively that she would be upset by it. Soon he would open his buggy shop. Then he might try to court her.

Then he'd make her forever his…if she let him, and therein lay the problem.

By the time lunchtime rolled around, *Dat* and Isaac were working with him to repair Martha's barn roof.

"You've done a *gut* job here, Eli," his *dat* said.

"We all worked hard. The *haus* looks better than it did," he admitted. Isaac and Jedidiah had painted the house shutters and the rest of the house exterior earlier in the week.

His father narrowed his gaze as he looked up the siding toward the roof shingles. "*Ja*, and after today, we should be done. Glad you waited before attempting to fix this yourself." *Dat* met his gaze. "Given the state of other things around this farm, the roof may not have been sturdy enough to take weight."

Eli shifted the ladder against the side of the barn. "I started to climb the ladder to fix a shutter but then thought of Horseshoe Joe."

"Joe learned a *gut* lesson." Samuel Lapp tightened his tool belt and reached out to push on the barn siding. "Looks like a couple of these boards are loose. Better fix these. Isaac, hold the ladder for Eli while I hammer in a few nails."

"*Ja, Dat.*"

Eli checked the ladder weight against the barn roof edge. Satisfied that it would hold, he climbed up and studied the condition of the roof shingles.

"Eli, how does it look?"

"Bad." Checking his nail bag, Eli saw that he had enough nails, but what he needed was the caulk gun. "Forgot caulk."

"I've got some in the buggy," his father said and left to retrieve it.

"Looks like it'll need replacing by next year, but we can patch her for now." Now that he saw its condition, Eli was leery about climbing onto the roof without some type of bracing. He came down a few rungs and smiled at his brother as he waited for his father to return with the caulk gun. "How's Nancy?" he asked casually.

Isaac grinned. "*Gut.* I'm going to meet her today."

"*Dat* know?"

"*Ja*, and he is fine with it."

"Has he met her yet?"

"*Nay*, but he will soon."

Eli studied his younger brother, worried that in his lovesick state he might be blinded to the girl's true self. He didn't want Isaac to get his heart broken. "I'm sure she's nice if you like her, but English girls are not like Amish—so be careful."

A myriad of emotions flickered across Isaac's expression. He looked as if he didn't know whether to be angry with his brother's warning or if he would take it as it was meant—an older brother's concern for a younger sibling.

Apparently, Isaac understood Eli's intent because his brow cleared suddenly and he nodded. "Nancy is a nice girl. She wants to meet our family. I thought I'd bring her by for Saturday supper."

That was two days away, Eli thought. "Did you tell *Mam*?"

"Not yet, but I will. I thought I'd ask her when I get home."

Eli smiled. "*Gut.* Knowing *Mam*'s loving heart, she'll be happy to have Nancy join us."

Isaac returned his grin. "I thought this, too."

Dat returned with the caulk gun and a new tube of caulk. Eli climbed back up the ladder to repair what he could safely reach. *Dat* and Isaac decided to check and fix, if necessary, the rest of the barn.

Martha came outside, bringing food and drink, and they stopped what they were doing to meet her.

Eli climbed down the ladder and took off his tool belt. *Dat* and Isaac came out of the barn and did the same before they all happily accepted the sweet iced tea and hot ham and cheese sandwiches that Martha had made for them.

"You spoil us, Martha," *Dat* said with a smile.

"You've been working hard," she said. "'Tis the least I can do."

Dat leaned to study the food items on Martha's tray. "Corn bread?" he guessed.

"*Ja.* And I bought you four samples of my jellies and jams that will be sold locally." She named three shops that they recognized, including Whittier's and Yoder's. "I think customers might be more inclined to buy my products if they tried them on crackers or my sweet corn bread."

"The corn bread you made this morning," Eli murmured.

Martha met his gaze. "*Ja.* Try a piece."

"I'd love to."

He saw that his father and brother were just as eager to taste it.

"Delicious!" *Dat* exclaimed. "What kind of jam is this?"

She blushed. "I call it sweet mixed berries. It's something new. I mixed strawberries, raspberries and gooseberries together. It smelled wonderful when I was making it, but I haven't actually tried it myself yet."

"You've got another winner," Eli declared before he took another bite.

He was delighted to see her expression light up with happiness.

They tasted all four jellies and jam and decided that all of them would sell well.

"I'm going to buy some of this for Katie," *Dat* said of Martha's hot pepper jelly.

"I have a fresh jar inside I can give you for all you've done."

Dat shook his head. "I'll not be taking any of your store-ready jellies or jams unless I can pay for it."

A twinkle entered Martha's eyes. "Then I'll go inside and get the lid for this jar. You can take this one home," she insisted.

His father laughed. "You sure know your mind," he said. "I know Katie and I will be enjoying hot pepper jam for breakfast tomorrow morning."

They went back to work while Martha went inside. She returned to her vegetable garden about an hour later. She seemed comfortable in his presence today, not like in the barn during the storm. As he'd thought, it was the lightning and thunder that had bothered her, not him.

And he didn't know how he felt about that, because despite his better judgment he cared for Martha, although apparently she still thought of him as only a friend.

Martha couldn't put Eli out of her mind as she watched the Lapps head home after a full day of work. Because of the barn roof, it was not the last. She'd been conscious of Eli as never before while he'd eaten and appreciated her corn bread and jelly. Her awareness of him had started even before they were caught in the barn together during that terrible rainstorm, and it had steadily intensified ever since.

Stop, she mentally scolded herself. *Stick with your plan to manage on your own.*

Eli was a good person and friend. He was always ready to help her whenever she needed him, but that didn't mean there could be feelings between them other than as friends and neighbors.

He wants to open a carriage shop. She smiled. He would be successful at the business, too. He was a hard worker who was thoughtful and considerate. He would do well with his customers, making sure they were satisfied. It wasn't the money he wanted most, but to do a good job and to provide a service to his community. She had to respect that.

Thoughts of Eli naturally made her think about her late husband. After he'd passed on, she'd moved out of their bedroom into one of the smaller rooms. In fact, she barely entered their former bedroom except to clean.

She still hadn't gone through Ike's belongings. Until now, she wasn't ready to face the task.

She'd do that first thing tomorrow morning. Tonight she would design a label for her jelly jars.

Seated at the kitchen table after dinner, Martha made notes and sketched design ideas. She could talk with Bob Whittier. He might know someone who could help her with her jar labels. She'd decided on a brand name: Martha's Best. It was an idea based on Eli's suggestion, yet it was short and memorable and she thought it would work well with any one of the designs she'd drawn. She'd ask Eli's opinion to make sure the name didn't come across as too bold.

On a separate clean sheet of paper, Martha jotted down the ingredients she'd need to keep the stores stocked with her products. She was determined to be successful. She had to be, or she would be looking for a job as a housekeeper or waitress, and while both were good jobs, neither one of them appealed to her.

Martha spent the rest of the evening preparing for future sales. She felt pleased when she came up with a final design and business plan that she was sure would work. That night, happy with her progress, she slept well for the first time in ages. The next morning, she woke up refreshed, ready to begin her day. And she would start it by cleaning out her late husband's belongings.

She enjoyed a breakfast of tea and toast, then went to clean out Ike's belongings from their old bedroom. There was a storage bench beneath one window. She lifted its wooden seat lid, and immediately the scent of her late husband rose up to overwhelm her. Images and happy memories flooded her mind. Love filled her heart, the love she'd once harbored for him when she was a new bride. Ike's clothes blurred as her eyes filled with tears. She lifted his belongings from the chest and set them carefully onto the end of the bed.

"Ike," she whispered brokenly as grief overcame her. She began to cry in earnest, for the loss of a good man, for the knowledge that he'd left this life when they'd not been on the best terms. He hadn't forgiven her for not getting pregnant after six months. Then after a year it seemed as if he'd no longer cared about having a child or for *her*. Would Ike have eventually come to accept and enjoy their childless marriage? Or would he have continued to ignore her, settling instead for buying fancy farm equipment and putting all his attention and enjoyment into farming as he had been during their last months together?

Sorrow made her chest tighten and brought a lump to her throat as she sorted Ike's clothing into neat piles of shirts, socks, underwear and trousers.

If only he had understood and believed that

she had wanted a baby as much as he did. If only, in the end, things had been different between them and she'd felt loved.

Chapter Fifteen

When Eli came to work alone the next morning, his arrival was later than usual. There wasn't much left to do at Martha's farm except the barn roof and a couple of other small tasks. As he maneuvered his buggy to park near the barn, he thought about the time he'd spent here...and how much he would miss seeing Martha every day.

He climbed down from his vehicle and stared at the house. The structure looked well kept with its newly painted working shutters, window trim and doors. Eli was pleased with all they had accomplished and for an amount that Martha could afford.

She hadn't been widowed a full year yet. Dare he tell her how he felt? Or would he frighten her by confessing his feelings for her? And what exactly did he feel? Friendship sure, but it was more. It was a feeling that told him that when she was ready, he wanted to pursue their relationship.

As he approached the house, he noticed that her windows were open, allowing the outside breeze to filter in. He headed toward the back door, raised his hand to knock but stopped when he heard soft sobbing inside. Eli moved to the window and saw Martha at the kitchen table. His gut wrenched as he realized that something had caused her pain.

"Martha," he said worriedly. She looked up, widened her eyes as she saw him in the window opening before she glanced away. He opened the door and stepped inside. "Martha, what's wrong?" he asked with concern as he closed it behind him.

Her tear-filled eyes made his stomach twist into a knot. And then he saw the pile of men's clothing on the chair next to her and he understood. "You cleaned out Ike's belongings."

"Ja." She gazed up at him with glistening brown eyes, and his heart melted. "It had to be done," she whispered. "I don't know why I didn't do it sooner."

He felt her pain as if it were his. It hurt, too, to realize that Martha had loved her husband so much that she was grieving for him still. She wasn't ready to move on, and even if she were, given the difference in their ages and his current inability to provide for her, Eli feared that he'd lost any chance of winning her heart.

"What are you planning to do with them?" he asked softly as he pulled out a chair and sat down across from her.

She blinked back tears. "I thought maybe Amos would want them. Do you think he'd like to have his *bruder*'s clothes?"

Eli gave her a gentle smile. "I'm sure he will." He hesitated. "Would you like me to take them to him?" Amos King was a longtime friend and neighbor who lived on the farm across the road from his father's.

"You'd do that?" She sniffed, wiped her eyes with her fingers.

"*Ja*, 'tis no inconvenience. Amos lives close by."

Martha rewarded him with a genuine smile that warmed him from the top of his head to his toe tips.

He stood, eager to please her, and she rose to follow. He held out his arms, and she retrieved the pile of men's clothing and came around the table to hand it to him. "I'll put these in the buggy," he said before he turned away.

"Eli," she called softly.

He halted on his way to the door and faced her. *"Ja?"*

"Danki."

He was glad to see that her sadness had eased. "'Tis my pleasure, Martha." It would always be his pleasure to help her.

Eli left to stow the clothing, which included shirts, pants and three hats—two straw and one black felt Sunday best—into the back of his vehicle. He returned to the house when he was done. He couldn't start work without checking on her one more time.

She stood near the stove. When she heard him come in, she turned to him. He was surprised and gratified to see a big smile on her face. "I put coffee on. I thought I'd make you something to eat." Her tone was pleasant, brisk.

He didn't have the heart to tell her that he'd already eaten. Besides it was hours ago when he'd eaten two of his mother's homemade butter biscuits.

"You don't have to go to any trouble for me." Although he wanted to stay and spend more time with her, he didn't want her to think she had to cook or do anything for him.

"'Tis no trouble." She was already taking out cooking utensils, dishes and pans. "Eggs? Pancakes? Waffles?"

He grinned at her, happy to be able to stay alone in her presence for a while longer. "I don't need all that." He pushed back the sudden sad thought that his time with her was limited and his work there almost over. He realized that he could see her every day, spend every moment with her and it would never be enough time.

If she was disappointed, she didn't show it. "I can make you eggs, and I have some muffins and corn bread left in the pantry."

"Perfect."

She looked pleased as she headed toward her food pantry. He watched her reach into her food stock and take out two plates.

His mouth watered in anticipation of her cooking. "Do you have any open jars of jelly?" He sat down at her kitchen table.

She beamed at him as she set the plates within his reach. "I'll get them from the refrigerator." She brought back five different kinds, which he eyed with delight.

"This is nice, Martha," he said after she'd fixed them both eggs, poured them each a cup of coffee and then taken the seat across from him.

She picked up a plate of baked goods and handed it to him. He grinned as he took a piece of corn bread and a sweet muffin, then reached for a knife and a jar of jam.

She smiled back, and at this moment all seemed right in Eli's world.

It didn't take Eli long to repair the last few items on his father's list or to install a back screen door, which wasn't on the list. When he was done, he decided to check Martha's fence line. He doubted that Amos had found the time, and Eli thought he could repair any breaks before her animals found another way to escape. Next time livestock got out of the pasture, he wouldn't be there to help her.

Isaac and Jedidiah arrived as he was checking the front fence line. Surprised to see them, he waved them over. "I didn't expect to see you here today."

Jedidiah shrugged. "I had some time, so I thought I'd stop by to see if you needed any help finishing up."

Eli looked at Isaac.

"I was done at home and I'll be seeing Nancy tomorrow, so I thought I'd come, too," their younger brother said. "Sarah and Gideon are at the house visiting with *Mam* and *Dat*. Poor Gideon didn't need someone else gawking at him."

Jedidiah laughed at Isaac's mention of someone gawking at his young son. "Gideon loves all the attention."

Isaac grinned at the boy's father. "He'll get plenty without us."

"I finished *Dat*'s list," Eli said. "And I installed a screen door."

Jed raised his eyebrows. "You bought Martha a door?"

Eli shrugged. "Thought she might like to leave the inside door open like *Mam* does on nice days."

Jedidiah nodded, and Eli was relieved that his older brother seemed to accept his reasoning behind his spending money on the door. "What can we help you with?" He frowned. "What are you doing *here*?"

"I thought while I was here I'd walk the fence line and fix any breaks so her animals won't get out."

"We can help you with that." No doubt, Jed was recalling Eli's story of chasing animals on Martha's farm. "Where do you want us to start?"

Eli directed each brother to a different area of the fence. Within an hour, the brothers had checked the fence and were satisfied that all of it was in good order.

"What about inside the house?" Isaac asked as they met in the barnyard. "Was there anything inside to be done?"

"I don't think so," Eli said. But he hadn't asked, had he?

Jedidiah looked skeptical. "Hard to believe given the condition of the outside. Shall we check with her before we leave?"

Eli agreed but then was tensely silent as

Jedidiah tapped on Martha's new screen door. Martha appeared, wiping her hands on a dish towel.

"Jed! Isaac! Eli, are you finished?" Throwing the towel over her left shoulder, she opened the door and invited them in. "Have you come for the balance owed?"

"Nay," Eli said. *"Dat* said there's no balance."

Martha looked puzzled as she glanced from him to Jedidiah and on to Isaac. "Then you've come to tell me that you're leaving."

Jedidiah spoke up. "We thought we'd check to see if there is anything that needs fixing inside."

Martha widened her eyes. "In the house?" She looked from Jed to Eli. Eli nodded. "There's nothing much. Maybe just a squeaky door."

"I can fix that for you," Jed offered. "Why don't you show me?"

While Martha left to show Jed the problem door, Eli stayed in the kitchen with his younger brother.

"This shouldn't take long," Isaac said.

"Ja." He stared in the direction where Martha and Jed had disappeared. He would have liked to be the one to help her. It bothered him that he hadn't offered first, but Eli knew that in the end the only thing that mattered was Martha's fixed door.

She and Jed returned from the other room

within seconds. "Nothing some greasing can't
fix," Jed told Eli. "Do you have any WD-40 left
at home?"

"Probably," Eli said. "*Dat* greases his farm
equipment with it." He turned to Martha. "I can
come back tomorrow to fix that for you."

She nodded. "That would be *gut*."

Eli left then with his brothers. Martha walked
them outside and waved from her front porch
as Jed drove away first with Eli and Isaac following. Eli was glad to have an excuse to return to the farm the next day. He wasn't ready
to stop seeing Martha, even if their friendship
stayed the way it was…even though he wished
for more from her.

On Saturday, the whole family gathered at the
Samuel Lapp farm. Noah and Rachel came with
their baby daughter. Jedidiah and Sarah arrived
shortly afterward with young Gideon. Jacob and
Annie were late as Annie and EJ had been napping and had overslept while Jacob had finished
a custom job at the forge. Eli had gone earlier
that morning to oil Martha's squeaky door, but
the task didn't take long and he was back home
within a half hour. He wished they were in a relationship that would have allowed him to invite her.

It was his sister Hannah's fifth birthday. *Mam*

had baked Hannah's favorite cake, and Jed and Sarah had brought two different flavors of ice cream. Annie had made potato salad for the occasion. Eli had teased Rachel earlier when he'd watched Noah trailing behind his wife carrying the huge stockpot of Amish chicken potpie she'd cooked.

"Feeding the whole congregation?" he'd teased as he put out his arms for his young niece.

"Only half of it," Rachel quipped with a smile as she handed him her daughter.

Eli studied his sister-in-law, pleased by what he saw. "You're looking well."

She glanced at her husband, who had reached her side. "Is there any reason why I shouldn't?" she asked, narrowing her gaze at Noah's guilty look.

"He saw the cradle," Noah admitted.

"I didn't say a word," Eli said.

Rachel beamed at him. "*Gut.* Please keep it that way. I want to tell the family."

"As you should." Eli turned Katy within his arms so that they were forehead to forehead then nose to nose. "Katy, girl, are your *eldre* treating you well? Or would you like to come live with your favorite *onkel*?" His little niece was adorable. He experienced a sudden intense longing for children of his own.

Rachel laughed. "This one is mine, Eli. Have

one of your own." She looked at him thought-fully. "After you settle down with the right girl."

Martha. Eli wondered if he would ever settle down. The only woman he wanted was Martha, and she was too much in love with her late husband to move on.

"I'm not ready to settle down," he said, hoping that his smile for Rachel appeared genuine. "I'll just have to settle for stealing this little one's attention."

"I think otherwise," Jedidiah whispered to him with a mysterious smile a short time later out of earshot of Rachel, who had left with Katy once again within her arms. "You like Martha King."

Eli scowled at him. "What makes you think that?"

"You've spend a lot of time with her. You bought her a door."

He raised his eyebrows and laughed. "Buying her a door means I'm smitten?"

"Smitten," his older brother said. "Telling choice of words."

"It is not!"

"And you ate meals with her."

Eli shrugged. "And so did Isaac and *Dat*."

"What did I do?" Isaac asked after hearing his name mentioned as he approached.

"You ate lunch with Martha," Eli said.

"Ja," he said, "as did *Dat* and you."

Eli shot his older brother a triumphant look. "I told you."

"Ja, but I'm sure you liked it more."

Isaac agreed, which earned him a scolding look from Eli. "He did."

"We're friends," was Eli's only answer.

Jedidiah flashed him a knowing look.

"Jed, stop. Installing a door and eating a couple of meals with Martha doesn't mean I'm in love with her."

"Hmm. He doesn't want to admit it, Isaac," Jed said with a half smile. He studied Eli with a knowing gaze. "Visiting Sunday is tomorrow. We'll see how the wind blows."

Isaac and Jedidiah nudged each other as they grinned at Eli.

"Lecherich," Eli muttered, calling them ridiculous.

"Who is being ridiculous?" their father asked as he joined them.

"Your other *soohns* here," Eli said. "They think they know everything, yet they don't have a clue."

Dat gazed at his boys with fond amusement. "That wouldn't stop them from making assumptions, *ja*?"

Eli smiled. *"Ja."* Leave it to *Dat* to see things as they were.

Their father turned to Isaac. "Where is this Nancy?" he asked with a smile.

"She'll be here. She had something to do for her *mam* first."

"A girl who thinks of her *mudder*," Dat said. "That is a *gut* trait in a *dochter*."

When Nancy arrived a short while later, Eli saw that his father's jaw might drop to the floor, but *Dat* managed to smile and hide his thoughts. Because Nancy looked like anything but a good daughter with her jet-black hair, heavily made-up eyes and lips covered with ruby-red lipstick. To give them credit, his family greeted the young woman warmly while they tried not to stare at her gold-ball lip piercing.

Eli studied his brother Isaac, noting how happy he was to have this young girl dressed in black and wearing a strange necklace here among his family.

"*Hallo*, Nancy," his mother greeted her with a smile. "We put out the food. Are you hungry?"

"I wouldn't mind eating." The girl, having heard that it was Hannah's birthday, had brought a gift. She handed the wrapped package to his mother. "For Hannah."

"Thank you, Nancy." Katie eyed the prettily wrapped package. "Isaac, why don't you get Nancy a plate and help her to get some food? Make sure you introduce her to the family."

"Ja, Mam." Isaac grinned at the dark-haired girl. "Come with me, Nance. You like cake? *Mam* bakes a *gut* birthday cake."

"Is it vegan?" Nancy asked, apparently concerned.

"Huh?" Isaac said. "I don't know what that is, but it's wonderful and I think you will like it."

"We must pray for him," his eldest brother, Jed, murmured fervently in Eli's ear.

Amused although he attempted to hide it, Eli looked at him with raised eyebrows. "Because she is different?"

Jedidiah shook his head. "Because she will hurt him."

Eli sighed, silently agreeing with his brother's assessment of Isaac's new English girlfriend. He knew what it was like to love the wrong woman, someone out of his reach, at least for now. But he would rather love a kind and God-loving widow who had everyone's best interests at heart than a girl who was not only not Amish but different from most *Englishers*.

Everyone in his family was kind and gracious to Nancy, and Isaac appeared happy. Eli was pleased that his family lived the way of the Lord, accepting others as they were, despite their differences. They were human and made mistakes, but they treated everyone as God would want them to.

Loving Martha wasn't wrong at all. It just wasn't the right time for them. He would have to wait until she was over her late husband before he told her of his feelings. Then when the time was right, if the Lord willed it, he would set out to court her…and win her heart.

Sunday morning, Eli ate breakfast with his family before they headed across the road to the farm belonging to the Amos Kings. Eli felt slightly anxious. His brothers' teasing the previous day concerned him. How had they guessed about his feelings for Martha? Was he really that transparent?

"What do you think of Nancy?" Isaac asked as they walked down their dirt lane toward the main road and the Amos King farm beyond.

"She seems nice," their younger brother Daniel said generously.

"She is nice," Isaac assured them, looking pleased. "I know she looks odd with her dark hair and lip piercing, but she is a *gut* person. We have a lot in common."

Eli and his mother exchanged looks. "You do?" his mother asked. "Like what?"

Isaac smiled as he glanced back at her. "We both love our families."

Mam smiled. "That is a fine quality in a person."

Isaac halted and waited for their youngest brother and sister to catch up.

"You help *Dat* on the farm," Eli said carefully. "How does she spend her day?"

"She waits tables at her mother's *coffe* shop after school."

"So she is a hard worker, too," *Dat* said as he walked next to *Mam*.

Eli hung back to trail behind, but he could hear everything said and he participated in the conversation. Daniel, Joseph and Hannah walked next to their father up in the front of the family group.

"When will you see her again?" Eli asked.

"Tomorrow night. She invited me to have dinner with her *mam* and *dat*."

"Will you be home afterward?" *Mam* asked casually.

"*Ja, Mam*, don't you worry. I'll be home. I told Jedidiah that I'd help out at the construction site tomorrow morning."

At Isaac's glance, Eli said, "Me, too."

The family reached the paved road and prepared to cross it, waiting for several cars and two trucks to pass. Martha King's buggy came into view briefly as she drew her horse to a halt as she waited for a car to pass before turning onto her brother-in-law's property.

Mam waved and called, "Martha!"

Martha smiled and returned the greeting. Her gaze settled on Eli before moving on.

Eli felt the sudden urge to pick up the pace. He wanted to get to Amos's, where he could casually spend time with Martha. He crossed the road and walked the newly graveled road with his family until they reached Amos and Mae King's farmhouse. Martha was climbing out of her parked buggy as he entered the yard.

"Martha," Eli murmured. As the members of his family split up to meet with friends and neighbors who had arrived before them, Eli headed toward Martha. He halted, changing his mind about approaching when a group of churchwomen beckoned to her. He shifted direction as she joined them, hurrying instead toward his brothers Jacob and Jedidiah, who were talking with Amos and John, his son.

Martha. What was he going to do about Martha? Maybe he should avoid her, but what if someone noticed? How would he feel if someone within the community asked him why?

Several girls within the community stood in the backyard visiting with one another. It wasn't long ago that he would have been content to stand among them, teasing them, being flattered by their attention. But they no longer held any interest—not even in the smallest way. There was only one reason why—Martha.

Chapter Sixteen

"Martha, you're looking well," Alta Hershberger said.

"That's kind of you, Alta."

"Not at all, just noting the truth."

Martha stood outside with a group of church-women after helping them to set out food and drink on a table in her brother-in-law's backyard.

"You seem to be managing well on your own," Miriam Zook said. "It must have been a rough winter for you."

"*Ja*, thanks to the *gut* company of Missy's daughter Meg, I did fine."

Missy Stoltzfus smiled. "She enjoyed staying with you. Ever since she was ill, Arlin has been worried about her. He was forced to face that she is doing well when she stayed with you and enjoyed herself."

"She's a lovely girl, Missy," Annie Lapp said. "All of your five daughters are."

Missy looked pleased.

"How are you managing financially?" Alta asked Martha. The woman was the resident busybody, but Martha took no offense, for she was pleased with what she'd accomplished during the past week.

"*Gut.* I've talked with several local shops in the area and three have agreed to sell my jams and jellies."

Alta frowned. "You are going into business? That doesn't seem wise."

"Her jams and jellies are delicious," Katie Lapp said, approaching from behind. The women moved to include her in the discussion. "Samuel brought home your hot pepper jelly and told me how *gut* it was. I was amazed after I tasted it. There was something about it that made me go back for more. I'm afraid I ate most of it."

Martha was delighted. "I'll send more over for you. Samuel wouldn't take a sealed jar, even after all he and your boys did for me. They did a wonderful job with the repairs to my house."

"'Twas their pleasure, I can assure you," Katie said.

"*Mam!*" Hannah Lapp appeared next to Katie. "Joseph fell and hurt himself. He is asking for you."

"How bad?"

"Skinned his knee and his elbows."

Katie shot each of the women a look of apology. "Excuse me while I attend to my youngest *soohn*."

"I hope he's all right," Martha said with concern.

"I'm sure he'll be fine."

As soon as Katie left, Mae exited her house and joined them. "Do you think we've enough food?" she asked with a worried look toward the food table.

Miriam Zook followed the direction of Mae's gaze. "Are you teasing? We have enough to feed our entire congregation plus that of the next church district," she assured her.

"Plenty of food," Alta said briskly, before the woman returned her attention to Martha. "Now, about this jelly business… Why would you want to go into business?"

"Why not?"

"Because it doesn't seem right."

"I sold my cakes and pies at Spence's Bazaar every week when I lived in Delaware," Sarah Lapp said. "My family depended on that money."

"And, Alta, didn't you sell your pickles and relishes for a time?" Miriam asked.

Alta made a sound like a *harrumph*. "That's different. I had two little ones to feed."

"And Martha has a large farm to maintain," Annie pointed out.

"It seems to me that Martha would be better off marrying again. She's been alone long enough."

"You never remarried, Alta," Miriam said.

"For me, it was different. I had both of my *dechter* and Martha has no one."

Martha was sad to be reminded again of the fact. "I don't think I'll ever marry again." Not after Ike. Not after John. And the only man who interested her was too young.

"We could find you a husband." Alta glanced about the yard as if searching for someone whom Martha could marry.

"Nay!" Martha exclaimed, horrified by the idea.

But Alta was determined. "Let's see…" Ignoring Martha's distress, the woman looked about the yard, her eyes gleaming as searched for a potential beau. "There."

Martha looked and was stunned to encounter Eli's blue gaze. He was crossing the yard with Jacob and Noah, heading toward the food. He flashed her a small smile as he continued on.

"Eli Lapp," Alta pronounced happily. "He's available and he needs to settle down."

"Nay," Martha whispered with a shake of her head.

"Stop interfering, Alta," Miriam scolded. "Mind your own business." She paused. "Unless you'd like us to find *you* a husband."

Alta raised her chin and stiffened her spine. "What? I'm only thinking of Martha's welfare."

Miriam shook her head. "Perhaps you should turn your attention toward husband hunting for Sally or Mary," she said, referring to Alta's daughters.

"Sally is seeing someone," Alta said in a snit. "Mary will find someone in time. She doesn't need me to help her."

The women in the group demanded more information about Sally Hershberger's sweetheart.

Martha had felt a tingling along her spine from the moment she and Eli had locked gazes earlier. She continued to feel the impact of his presence in the yard.

"Martha." Annie drew her aside. "Don't pay my aunt any mind. Her heart is in the right place, but she still manages to create problems for everyone she comes in contact with. Her husband died when her girls were young. She was lost and angry until she finally got herself together for Sally and Mary. I often wonder if she would have married again if someone had bothered to ask. Instead she's made everyone's business her own. I think that she intimidates most of the men she encounters. She's a forceful woman, and at times even I'm frightened of her."

"Annie..." Martha was uncomfortable but felt as if she had to tell her friend. "About Eli..."

Her friend smiled. "You like him."

"You can tell?" she gasped.

"Not for certain, but I thought you might. You both seem so easy around each other."

That was news to Martha, that Eli felt easy in her company. "Please do not say a word to anyone. Not even Jacob. I'm too old for Eli, and he has plans of his own. I want what's best for him. I need him to be happy."

Annie looked thoughtful. "I won't mention it to anyone," she promised.

"Not even to Jacob?"

"I don't like keeping things from my husband." Annie settled her interlocked fingers on her pregnant belly. "But for your sake, I'll keep your secret for now."

"Danki." Martha hadn't known how tense she'd been until Annie's promise made her relax with tremendous relief.

"You should tell Eli. What if he feels the same as you?"

Martha nodded. "If I come to believe that he feels the same, I will tell him."

Annie grinned. *"Gut."* She glanced behind her. "Because he's coming this way."

"Who? Eli?" The thought made her heart start to pound.

"Ja. With Jacob."

Martha drew a sharp breath, and her hands felt clammy.

"Hallo, husband," Annie greeted Jacob with a loving smile. "Eli, I hear you've finished Martha's repairs. She told me what a *gut* job you did."

"I wasn't the only one who worked on her *haus,"* Eli said, approaching from behind Martha. "It was a Lapp family project."

Eli's nearness made her vibrate the length of her from her nape to her toes. Searing her friend with a warning glance, Martha faced the twin brothers.

"You did more than the lion's share, Eli." Martha gazed up at him, astonished by how handsome he was and how much he affected her heart and peace of mind.

"Oh, dear. Here comes Alta!" Annie gasped.

Eli frowned, and Martha knew she needed to escape before Alta said something to embarrass her and Eli.

Martha explained, "She doesn't approve of me selling jellies."

"She does have strange notions about what's right and wrong," Jacob admitted.

"Let's go for a short walk, *ja?*" Annie suggested.

"Are you sure you're up to it?" Jacob asked his wife.

"I have at least another month before the birth of our daughter. I'm feeling particularly well today."

Martha felt surprised by her friend. "You know it's a girl?"

"*Nay.* It's just a feeling that I have."

There was tenderness in his expression as Jacob smiled at his wife. "I don't mind one way or another. I just want our child to be healthy and well."

"Did you eat?" Annie asked him. "I saw you by the food table."

Jacob shook his head. "Just checking out the selection."

"Why don't we get something to eat?" Eli suggested. "We can sit and enjoy our meal under that tree there." He gestured to one of several tables that were set up in the shade.

"I should see if Mae needs any help." Martha wanted to stay and spend time with Eli, but she didn't want to give Alta or anyone else fodder for gossip.

"I will see you later," she said before she walked away.

"We'll see you later, Martha," Annie said. "Come. Let's eat. The woman has things to do. Maybe she'll come back to eat dessert with us."

Now that the Lapps were no longer daily working visitors, Martha realized how much she'd come to enjoy having Eli and his family working about the yard and house. Her days now were silent and solitary. She missed Eli more than ever and there was nothing she could do about it, except hope that with the passing of time she could move on and forget the handsome young man who had somehow changed her.

The last time she and Eli had conversed was during last visiting Sunday. They'd spoken briefly but for the most part she'd hung back, not wanting the others to recognize her deep feelings for Eli.

All day long, she'd felt him watching her from the other end of the yard. While she'd joined Annie, Jacob and Eli for dessert after the midday meal, she'd kept her distance afterward, leaving quickly after she'd eaten her pie to visit with other community church members.

Fortunately for her, Alta Hershberger had seemed to give up the idea of finding her a husband. She didn't know what she would have done if Alta mentioned Eli as her potential husband one more time. Martha knew that Eli was a man she liked, but that didn't mean she should harbor secret dreams of a life together.

The weather was hot and humid. The heat hung heavily in the air, sapping her strength. She'd needed to make more jellies to sell since the stores had already let her know that they'd soon be looking to restock. Fortunately, Meg and her four sisters had helped with jam making this past Monday. They'd cooked up three different kinds of jellies and jam, and now the jars sat in bright, colorful rows in her pantry, on her kitchen table and along the length of her kitchen countertop.

She'd put on the wash first thing that morning and hung the clothes out to dry when they were ready. Martha went to check the degree of dampness and realized that the towels and sheets were never going to dry in the day's humidity. She unpinned the laundry, brought it inside to put into the gas clothes dryer. While her wash spun dry in her machine, Martha left the house to check her vegetable garden. The plants were growing nicely. In a few weeks, there would be cherry tomatoes to pick and soon after that the first of her green peppers. The day was unusually warm. She was perspiring profusely by the time she headed back to the house. Her clothes stuck to her body as she walked. Martha noted the haze in the air and decided that there'd be a thunderstorm by midnight.

That night, she ate a simple supper of iced tea, potato salad and leftover fried chicken, which she'd made for herself two days previously. Afterward she went to sleep in the small room where she'd slept since her husband's passing. It didn't matter that his belongings were gone from their bedroom. She was more comfortable in her room with its single bed and wooden rocking chair.

She opened a bedroom window and was glad to allow in a soft breeze. Thunder rumbled in the far distance as Martha got ready for bed. The cooler air and the distant noise were soothing and too far to be distracting. If there was lightning in the air, she couldn't see it yet. She fell asleep, believing that the storm would miss her farm, happy that the air had cooled off enough to make her bedroom comfortable to sleep.

The rainstorm came with a vengeance about midnight. Martha shot up, wide-awake, her heart pumping wildly, after a particularly loud thunder boom. From her bed, she gazed toward the window and saw multiple flashes of bright light followed by heavy rumblings of thunder. Her heart raced as she climbed out of bed to close the window and to get a better look at the storm's intensity. Should she reach out and close the shutters?

She gasped, backing away, as lightning zig-zagged across the sky. There would be no opening that window a second time. She flinched at the thunder that followed the bright flash of light, then watched with amazement as the rain began to fall harder and faster, a heavy downpour that came in seconds, immediately flooding the yard below.

I hope my garden survives this rain. The wind picked up, gusting across the yard and house. Martha feared for her trees and bushes that were vulnerable in the open, liable to be uprooted if the rain and wind continued as they were. Lightning glowed, illuminating the yard below. She saw the trunk of a solitary tree bending in the stiff breeze.

There was no way she'd be able to go back to sleep. Throwing on a robe, she went downstairs for a glass of iced tea and to watch the thunderstorm from the first level of the house.

A sharp crack of loud noise startled her. Gasping with fear, she hurried to the window in time to see that lightning had struck her barn, causing the wooden structure to burst into flames.

Crying out, she ran outside, oblivious to her state of dress and the pouring rain that drenched her within seconds. She stared at her burning barn, wondering what to do. How she was going to get help. Perhaps her neighbors had heard the noise and seen the fire.

She gazed in helpless horror as flames rushed up from the building's roof, her heart pounding, ignoring the rain, the lightning and thunder raging around her. The rain had slowed, but the wind blew what little fell against her face and neck.

The animals! She ran to the barn, shoved hard to open the door, her adrenaline pumping. Then she urged those animals inside the structure out into the night, praying that they wouldn't be struck by lightning or spooked by the thunder.

The rain tapered to a drizzle as the fire burned hotter and hotter. *Nay!* she thought, *Keep raining!* It was her only hope of extinguishing the flames.

She shuddered. Her late husband's new farm equipment was in that barn. She could feel the heat; it seared her skin even from across the yard. She no longer felt wet, but hot and damp and scared.

Lord, please help me.

And then they arrived in buggies and wagons, in cars and trucks—her neighbors and friends and other church families coming to battle the fire they must have glimpsed in the distance.

The Lapps came, including Eli. She'd never been happier to see them, all of them. She bent her head and sent the Lord a quick prayer of thanks.

Chapter Seventeen

Eli stared at the barn in shock and concern as his *dat* drove the buggy down Martha's driveway. It appeared as if everyone around for miles had come to fight the fire. Rick Martin had received the news from Bob Whittier, who had received word from the Jones family across the street from Martha's farm. Bob had alerted his family and Martha's relatives, the Amos Kings, across the road. When he'd learned that the fire was at Martha's, Eli thought he'd go crazy with worry. He was eager to get to her, to be available in her time of need. He wouldn't rest until he saw for himself that she was all right.

He jumped out of the buggy before his father had stopped it completely. He vaguely heard his mother calling his name, but he kept going. He couldn't wait to see her. The scene before him was chaos. There were people running this way and that, filling buckets from the water pump in the yard. Someone had started a bucket brigade. As he approached the water line, he passed Rick Martin, who was talking earnestly in his cell phone with what must be dispatch with the local fire department.

Eli spied Martha in the middle of the bucket brigade. He rushed to her side, wanting, needing to get close. "Martha!" He tugged her from the line so that they could talk, and to his surprise she went willingly. She looked a lovely mess with wet hair, dirty nightwear and soot on her cheek and across her forehead.

"Eli!" She brightened as if glad to see him, and his heart kicked into fast gear.

"Are you all right?"

"I'm fine." But she didn't look fine. Until he'd grabbed her, she had appeared stunned and slightly out of it, handing buckets to the next one in line automatically.

She wore no nightcap, probably because of the hot weather. Her hair was a gorgeous mess without pins to hold it up, and it flowed down her back in a tangle of wetness, mud and grass. He doubted she was even aware of how she looked, and he knew she'd be horrified if she'd known. He wanted nothing more than to take her into his arms and hold her until the fire was put out and her distress subsided.

"Were there animals inside?" he asked.

She gave a jerky nod. "I opened the barn door, and I think all of them ran out."

"Come," he urged her. "My *mam* is here. Go and stay with her. Rest a few minutes. You look as if you're about to fall down." He waved his mother over.

Mam immediately came, frowning as she noted Martha's condition and the devastation in the young widow's expression.

"*Mam*, take care of her, please," he beseeched, and his mother flashed him a surprised glance as she assured him that she would.

"I'm fine. I can go back and help," Martha insisted, but she looked anything but well.

"Let's go inside," his mother urged. "You're soaked through. There isn't anything you can do now. The firefighters are on their way."

The sound of fire engine sirens blasted loudly into the night.

"See? They're here. Please, Martha, go with my *mam*." The arrival of the fire department must have reassured her. He saw Martha nod, and he met his mother's glance, grateful as *Mam* placed her arm around Martha's shoulders and walked with her to the farmhouse.

With a sigh of relief, Eli turned his attention to the fire. As he drew closer to the barn, he heard a soft bleating sound—the cry he recognized as belonging to Millicent, the goat he'd helped Martha capture. Despite protests of those around him, he ran into the burning barn. Immediately he felt the intense heat. The smell of the fire and smoke was strong. He had to find Millicent quickly or succumb to smoke inhalation or flame himself.

And then he saw the frightened animal in a corner of her stall. She hadn't escaped through the open barn door. There was no time for him to do anything but snatch up the animal and carry her outside to safety.

"Eli!" Martha screamed. She stood on the back stoop, her eyes wide, her mouth trembling with anxiety. His mother came out of the house beside her and placed an arm around Martha's shoulders, drawing her close.

He had set the goat down and hurried to where Martha stood. "Millicent," he gasped.

She blinked back tears. "You shouldn't have gone inside. You could have been killed!"

"I'm fine." He flashed the two women a smile of reassurance. How could he explain that he had to rescue Millicent? She was a part of his happy memory of his and Martha's animal chase.

He glanced back at the barn and sobered. "The farm equipment," he said. "I'm afraid it's ruined."

"Equipment doesn't matter. What matters is

life—*your life*," she said. He saw something on her face that startled him and gave him hope. He caught glimpses of concern…worry…*love*.

"Martha, I—" He wanted to take her into his arms and tell her that she had nothing to worry about. He would always be there for her. "We need to talk later. But for now I've got to go."

"Eli—"

"Martha, *please*." He sought help from his mother. *"Mam…"*

"Come." Katie Lapp gently urged Martha back inside.

"I'm sorry." A man dressed in fire gear approached. "You'll have to move these vehicles. You!" the man said, pointing at Eli. "We're shorthanded tonight. Can you assist?"

Eli didn't hesitate. "Yes, I can help." He searched for his brothers. Spying them, he shouted, "Jed, Noah, Jacob! The firefighters need our assistance."

His brothers rushed to lend a hand, grabbing to help with the hose attached to the tanker truck.

Less than an hour after the fire truck had arrived, the flames were extinguished. Eli stared at the darkened building before heading toward the house. *Thank God*.

Martha stared at her burned barn through her kitchen window and wondered where she would house her livestock. Her sheep had already taken shelter in the lean-to Ike had once used to store his old plow. It was the same building her sheep migrated to when seeking shade during the extreme heat of the late summer afternoons. But that structure was barely big enough for her lambs.

Her horses had escaped from the pasture but hadn't gone far. Someone had rounded them up and brought them to safety on the house lawn. Her mare. Her gelding. Her three draft horses. They stood nearby, hitched to trees in her backyard.

The area around the barn was muddy from the rain and the firemen's hose. Her chickens were scattered in all directions, but Martha felt too tired to go outside after them. She realized there wasn't much she could do. Katie Lapp had been kind and caring, offering to help her change out of her muddy clothes. That she still wore her nightgown and robe shocked and embarrassed her. At Eli's mother's urging, she'd gone to her room to change. When she returned, Katie was on the back porch, but she'd left a fresh pot of steaming tea on the kitchen table. She turned from the window and stared at the teapot, hankering for a cup but aware that there were things that needed to be decided. *What to do next?*

Sarah Lapp, Eli's sister-in-law, rapped on her

back door and entered the room. She had come with Jedidiah and had joined the bucket brigade. "Martha? Are you well?"

Martha managed a small smile as she turned to her. "I'm fine." But she was exhausted and felt numb.

"Let me pour you a cup of tea," Sarah offered, regarding her with blue eyes filled with concern.

"Danki." Martha sat at the table, stared into space. All she could envision was Eli running into the burning barn to rescue her milk goat. She'd never been so terrified in her life. If anything bad had happened to him, she didn't how she would have coped. She closed her eyes. *Because I love him.*

"Here." Sarah set a cup of tea in front of her.

"Everyone is all right, *ja*?"

Sarah nodded. "No one was hurt in the fire."

"Thanks be to God." Martha shuddered, hugged herself with her arms.

"Drink your tea," Sarah ordered kindly.

She obeyed, sipping on the tea, which was made exactly to her liking. The hot sweetened brew revived her. "I'm sorry," she apologized. "Seems like everyone is always coming to my rescue."

"There is nothing to apologize for. Life happens, and we all pull together in times of need." Jedidiah's wife poured herself a cup of tea and sat down across from her. "We're happy to help. You've helped all of us when we needed you." Sarah smiled. "You brought us food and helped clean my house after Gideon was born."

That didn't seem like much. It certainly didn't seem like the same thing. She said as much to Sarah.

Sarah reached across the table to cover her hand with her fingers. Martha felt the woman's warmth and caring. Her friendship and kind words went a long way to making her feel better.

"Danki," she murmured to the young woman, and Sarah squeezed her hand. The Lapp family was always there for her. Eli seemed to show up whenever she needed him.

Suddenly she needed to see him more than she needed to breathe. *Eli.* She loved him. She couldn't tell him, but she could be there whenever he needed her. *I love him.* And she was both overjoyed and saddened by the realization that she was that far gone on him. But she couldn't let him know.

Eli glanced about the activity-filled yard in search of Martha. He didn't see her anywhere, and he became alarmed. If anything had happened to her...

He hurried toward the house, bumping into his *dat* as he went.

"*Soohn*, the fire is out. Where are you going in such a hurry?"

"Martha—" he began, panic settling in.

Dat studied him and said quietly, "She's in the house."

Eli closed his eyes as he released a sigh of relief. "*Dat*, I—"

"Go. Not much to do here but clean up, and it's late. We'll come back tomorrow to finish the job." He paused. "Don't be too long. Your mother will be worried sick, and everyone is tired."

Eli nodded and continued toward the farmhouse. He knocked on the door as he did when working there and entered without waiting for Martha to come.

"Martha!" he called.

A red-haired woman at the stove turned, and Eli saw that it was his sister-in-law. "Sarah, where's Martha?"

"She just went outside." Sarah gazed at him knowingly. "We just had tea. I'm making another pot. Would you like some?"

He shook his head. "I didn't see her."

"You must have missed her."

"She's all right?" he asked Sarah.

"*Ja*, she is fine. Tired, in shock. She's lost her barn and all that new farm equipment. Her animals are still running around, and she knows she needs to gather them, but she's so tired."

"Jedidiah, Jacob and Isaac are rounding up her livestock now. Jacob said that Joe has room in his barn for her cattle and draft horses."

"That's *gut*. Jed and I can house her chickens." Sarah poured water into a teapot and added a tea ball of loose tea leaves.

"Will you tell her I was asking about her?" Eli said.

Sarah gestured toward the door behind him. "Why don't you tell her yourself?"

He turned and through the screen saw her standing there. She had changed clothes. She was neatly dressed with her hair rolled and pinned under a white *kapp* as if it weren't three o'clock in the morning. Their gazes met, locked.

"I was worried," he said.

"I was terrified when you ran into the barn."

His spirits rose. "We'll all help," he said, "with your animals. Horseshoe Joe will house your cattle and draft horses."

"Jed and I will take your chickens until a coop can be built for them," Sarah added, reminding him that she was listening.

"You've all been wonderful. *Danki*."

"It's the middle of the night—you should be asleep."

Martha managed a weak smile. "We should all be asleep, but fate had other plans for us."

"Thank the Lord that no one was hurt," Sarah

said as she poured another cup of tea and gestured for Martha to take it.

"*Dat* wants to leave, but I'll be back tomorrow."

"You've done so much here, Eli. It doesn't seem right that you've had to come back and work here."

He saw her sway on her feet. "Sit down, Martha," he beseeched softly, "before you fall down. I will be back tomorrow." He gestured for Sarah to follow him so that he could talk with her privately. "Who has Gideon?" he asked her.

"My cousin Josie."

"Will you be able to stay with her tonight?"

Sarah nodded. "I can, but I think it would be better if we take her home with us. It will do her *gut* to be away from here for a while. I'll bring her back after she's had a rest." She hesitated. "What time will you be back tomorrow?"

Eli shrugged. "Not too early. It's late and none of us has had much sleep."

"I'll bring her back after ten thirty."

Eli nodded, then glanced toward the woman at the kitchen table. She stared ahead as if in a daze. Martha looked down then, lifted and sipped from teacup. He decided it was a good time to approach her. "Sarah is going to take you home with her," he said softly. "I'll see you back here tomorrow morning."

"There's no need—"

"Martha," he said quietly, his voice firm. "Please go with Sarah. My *bruders* will see to your animals. There is nothing else you can do. I'll feel better knowing that tonight you'll be in Sarah's capable hands. You'll get a better night's sleep away from this place."

"I don't want to impose—"

"You can never be an imposition," Sarah assured her. She went to the table and topped off her teacup; then she took the seat across from Martha and sipped her tea. "We'll enjoy a few quiet moments while we finish our tea, and then I'll help you pack a few things to take with you tonight. *Ja?*"

Martha looked from Sarah to Eli, and Eli saw indecision in her eyes. He begged her with his gaze to go. "Please," he mouthed.

She sighed and closed her eyes. "All right. I'll go with Sarah."

He grinned, pleased that tonight, at least, she'd be safe and he wouldn't have to worry about her fretting over her situation alone. "*Dat* is waiting for me, Martha, but I will see you tomorrow morning."

"*Gut* night." Her expression softened as she gazed at him.

Warmth filled his heart as he smiled at her. "Sleep well, Martha Jane."

* * *

Later that morning Eli was in the barnyard as Sarah brought Martha home. He stood at the fence, gazing out over the empty pasture. Hearing the sounds signaling Sarah and Martha's arrival, he pushed back from the fence and met them as Sarah parked the buggy close to the house. The scent of smoke and fire hung heavily on the day's breeze. It appeared as if steam still rose from the blackened ruins of the barn, but Eli realized that it was only the temperature and humidity that hovered over the damaged structure.

Eli came to Martha's side of the vehicle and extended a helping hand. "Did you get any sleep?" he asked.

She nodded as he helped her down. "The bed at Sarah's is extremely comfortable."

He noticed the dark circles under her eyes and turned to his sister-in-law. "How much sleep?"

"Not nearly enough," Sarah said. "I heard her moving about after only a couple of hours. She wanted to come here right away. Thankfully, I managed to convince her to eat breakfast first. I told her she'd need strength for when she gets home."

"You've been very kind," Martha said sincerely. Her gaze immediately settled on the barn. Her brow crinkled as if she was wondering what to do next. He felt her shudder before she hugged herself with her arms.

"We'll hold a barn raising to build a new barn," he said, wanting to draw her into his embrace.

"Everyone has done so much already."

"As you have done for others," Sarah reminded her. "Helping out Annie and me after our babies were born. Surpassing others in making items for the mud sale."

"I haven't done anything anyone else hasn't done."

"Yet it bothers you to accept help when you're used to giving," Eli said. "Are you that determined to do things on your own?"

Martha hesitated. *"Ja."* She turned to Sarah. *"Danki* for opening your home to me."

"I wish you'd stay longer," Sarah said with concern. "Gideon is taken with you."

Martha smiled, and Eli saw a tiny spark in her eyes that he recognized as pleasure. "He's a bright little boy. You are truly blessed to have him."

"Ja, the Lord blessed me with him and Jed." Sarah stood beside her buggy. "I should go. Come and stay with us again. Tonight."

"I'll be all right here at home." But Martha seemed pleased by Sarah's invitation. "I have to decide what to do."

Sarah nodded. "I understand." She climbed into her buggy and said, "Don't be a stranger, Eli. You haven't been around to visit in a while."

He smiled. "I'll stop by later today or early tomorrow." Eli was conscious of Martha beside him as Sarah drove away from the house and headed toward home.

"It was nice of her to have me," Martha said quietly.

"I'm glad she did. I was worried about you." He couldn't take his eyes off her. She shot him a look. Something strong passed between them, something that was obvious and exciting as well as scary.

"Martha," he began.

"Ja?" She glanced at him sideways as she ran her hands up and down her arms.

He frowned as he felt her shiver. "Are you cold?"

She shook her head, left him to walk toward what was left of her barn. "I can barely believe this happened."

He followed her. She stopped. When he reached her side, he gave in to the urge to place a hand on her shoulder. He heard her draw a sharp breath as she turned to face him.

"Eli…"

"Martha, I care about you."

"You shouldn't."

He furrowed his brow as disappointment made his chest hurt. "Why not?"

"I'm too old for you."

He gave her a tender smile. "*Ja*, you must be a hundred at least."

She scowled at him. "I'm serious, Eli. I'm nearly seven years older than you. You need someone your own age."

"I want to court you."

She gasped, pulled back. "*Nay*, you don't."

"We're more than friends," he said. "You like me, too."

She shook her head. "We're just friends," she insisted, but her gaze skittered away briefly.

"I don't believe you," he said softly, running his hand down her arm to grasp her fingers. "We're more than friends. Deny that you care for me, that you were worried about me when I ran into the barn."

Emotions warred in her expression. He could see that she wanted to deny it, to fight what she was feeling inside, but she couldn't. He felt her soften. He still held her hand.

"Martha?" he prompted quietly.

"*Ja*, I was concerned!" she burst out, jerking her hand away as if needing to break the contact. "I've come to know you during your work here.

Yes, we're friends, and I was worried. Wouldn't you be worried about a friend?"

"And that's all I am to you? Truly?" Eli watched her carefully, hoping for some sign that would betray her true feelings. He couldn't believe that she didn't feel as he did.

"Ja." Her clipped one-word emotionless answer cut him like a knife.

"You want me to leave?"

She nodded.

"Why, if we're only friends?"

"Because you don't feel as I do." Martha faced him, her brown eyes filled with compassion, concern. Her expression and answer finally convinced him. "You're young. You have plans for opening your own business. You've been working hard for that. Go and fulfill your goal of opening up a carriage shop. There are many girls within our community that you can pick from when you're ready to wed. I'm a widow with a farm and a burnt barn." Her voice caught. "I have my own life to live."

A rumbling on the dirt lane drew his and Martha's attention as a black town car drove up to the house and parked. The driver turned off the engine and got out of the vehicle. The man had dark hair and tortoiseshell-rimmed glasses, and he wore a dark suit, white shirt and dark tie.

Spying him and Martha, he approached. He addressed Eli. "Ike King?"

Eli shook his head. "Eli Lapp. Can we help you?"

The man turned his attention to Martha. "Are you Mrs. King?"

Martha nodded. "Yes," she said, speaking in clear English for his benefit. "How may I help you?"

"I understand there was a fire here last night." The man's gaze widened as it settled on the burned building.

Word traveled fast, Eli thought. 'That's right. Lightning struck the barn."

The man transferred his stern gaze to Martha. "It looks bad."

"Bad enough. Why do you ask?" Eli said. "Who are you?"

The suit looked at him. "I'm Jonathan Pierce from People's Resident Bank, which financed Mr. King's farm equipment. Can you tell me where Mr. King is? I'd like to talk with him."

"I'm afraid I can tell you where he is, but you won't be able to speak with him." Worry had clouded Martha's brow when the man mentioned the new farm equipment. "My husband passed away in November."

Jonathan Pierce appeared disturbed by the news. "There is a payment coming due on the equipment. We heard about the fire and wanted to make sure your circumstances haven't changed."

Eli stared at the man. "The payment is not due yet, but you came because you received news of the fire?" It didn't make sense to him, but then he wasn't an English bank representative. What kind of arrangement did Ike have with this bank?

Pierce nodded. "You will be able to continue making payments?" he asked Martha.

"She will," Eli chimed in before Martha could answer. He didn't care for the way the banker spoke to Martha.

"Good." The man's brow cleared. "I don't want to foreclose unless I have to."

"Foreclose?" Martha said, clearly at a loss.

The banker raised an eyebrow. "Foreclosure is starting proceedings to take property when someone gets behind in his loan payments." He eyed the barn, and his expression softened with compassion as his gaze settled again on Martha. "I'm sorry. I thought he would have told you. Your husband used the house as collateral."

Martha turned pale. "I see."

"You have forty days to make the next payment on your loan." The man named a figure that made Martha tense. She appeared unworried, but Eli was close enough to her to feel it.

Pierce turned and without saying a word opened his car door.

Eli stopped him, "Jonathan Pierce," he called. "Will you make us a copy of the loan documents?"

Looking surprised by the request, the man nodded. "I'll get them into the mail to you today."

"Thank you," Martha said quietly.

The banker took his leave without once looking back.

"Eli." Martha turned to him, looking worried. "Ike mortgaged the house."

"*Ja*, it seems that way."

"What am I going to do?"

Eli smiled reassuringly. He wanted to draw her close to comfort her, but he knew after their recent conversation that she wouldn't welcome it. "Don't *ya* mean what is our community going to do?" He dared to reach for her hand again, and this time he gave it a gentle squeeze before he released it. "We're going to raise enough money to pay off your loan."

Her eyes filled with tears, and he groaned, giving in to the urge to draw her into his arms. He felt her shudder, and he tightened his embrace. It felt good to hold her. He wished that she cared for him as he did her and that he had the right to hold her every day of their lives. *She does have strong feelings for me.* But he was aware that she was determined to fight them.

The community would pay off her loan, Eli thought. Build her a new barn. And he would open his business and then ask to court her. How could she say no to him then? Just because of a few years' age difference? If she clung to that reason, he would convince her that it didn't matter. He could name several married couples with large differences in age, and they were happy together. As he reluctantly released her, he offered up a silent prayer that the Lord would bless his and Martha's union as He had for his brothers and their spouses. With God on his side, he would surely be happily married by this time next year.

He stepped back to put distance between them. The best way to win this woman's heart was to give her the space to realize what she was missing. "Let's take a closer look at what's left of the barn," he said briskly.

Chapter Eighteen

News spread fast, and within a week the Happiness church community came together to plan a fundraiser for her. Martha was extremely grateful; she didn't want to lose her house and property. She thought about going home to Indiana to start over, but her place was here in Happiness. *Where Eli is*.

Besides, she'd received a letter in the mail from her parents only yesterday. Its contents made her realize that she couldn't go home again. Ironically, the letter had come at the same time as her copy of Ike's loan agreement with People's Resident Bank. She'd opened the bank envelope first and been shocked as she read through the document. She didn't completely understand the fancy legal words, but she understood the gist of the agreement. And she definitely understood the five-figure loan balance.

Numerous times over the course of the past week, she'd looked up to the heavens and asked Ike why. Why would he buy equipment they couldn't afford? *Why did you risk our farm— our home—for something that was impressive and nice but something we certainly didn't need?* Now all she had left was burned metal and a huge debt.

Twenty thousand dollars! It was foolish of you, Ike. Was that why he hadn't told her? She was his wife; their relationship should have been a partnership. But then things between them had gone from bad to worse.

Just at a time when she was seriously considering going back to Indiana, her mother's letter put an end to the notion. As the shock of the loan papers still vibrated through her being, Martha had opened her letter from home. What she'd read had made her heart tighten and her body tense. She'd read the letter once and then again, trying to absorb the letter's contents.

Dear Martha,
I hope you are managing well enough on your own. I was so sorry to hear about Ike's death. You were so happy on the day that you married him that I can't imagine what you are feeling now. I know it's been months since his funeral. I'm sorry that we

*couldn't attend. There were things going on
here at home that prevented us from leaving. I can't go into these things now, but I
hope you understand that we wanted to be
with you. We prayed for you every day and
still continue to do so.*

*I have news, which may or may not
upset you. I'd like to think that after all this
time—and your marriage to Ike—that this
won't bother you at all. But I felt you should
know. I didn't want you to hear it from anyone else, for you know that I love you.*

*John Miller has returned home, Martha.
He is a changed young man. Do you know
that he finally joined the Amish church? He
asked about you. He feels bad about the
way he left you...*

The news isn't just that John is back,
dochter, *but that he is married now. He is
happy, and I'm sure you want that for him
despite the fact that he broke your heart.
He did break your heart, didn't he? I wasn't
sure because I never saw you cry after he
left.*

*So maybe this news won't upset you after
all, and that is for the best. You see, Martha, John married someone you know—
Ruth. Ja, he married your sister. Ike was
still alive when they wed, and we didn't tell*

you as you were pleased with your new husband and we didn't want to spoil things for you. Ruth is so happy with John. I hope you will understand our decision not to tell you or invite you to the wedding. I trust that the Lord will once again make things right for you. I know you must feel lonely as a young widow, but I'm certain that you will find someone else to love and marry.

Dochter, *Ruth and John are expecting their first child. I didn't receive word from you and Ike, but I hope you have a baby of your own. There is nothing like loving a child.*

Please know that I think of you every day. Maybe someday you can come for a visit or we can come there. It may not be for a while as there is Ruth and John's baby to consider. We all miss and love you, and we wish only the best for you. Take gut *care of yourself.*
Mam

Martha had finished the letter with her eyes filled with tears. It was true that after John had left, her parents and family had never seen her cry. She'd fought to be strong. She hadn't wanted to upset them. But whenever she'd been alone in the room she shared with Ruth or out walking by herself across the farm fields, she allowed free rein to her emotion until she cried herself out.

Another reason to avoid Eli Lapp, she thought. She wouldn't be hurt a third time. If she could lose the interest of John Miller and her own husband, she was sure to lose Eli's interest.

Returning to Indiana was out of the question, Martha thought as she entered the building where the community was holding the first day's fundraiser for her. The last thing she wanted was to see John and Ruth together. Her mother was right; she did want John and her sister to be happy. *But together?* She felt betrayed not once but twice, and now by the both of them.

Martha stood in the middle of the local fire hall and eyed her surroundings with amazement. Her fellow church community members had pulled out all the stops for what was to be a two-day fundraiser to pay off her loan. Today was the first day of two Amish auctions. Everyone she knew had pitched in to set up for the event, even young Hannah Lapp, who was helping her cousins—the five Arlin Stoltzfus girls, including Meg, Charlie and their oldest sister, Nell.

Mae and Katie Lapp were arranging craft items on the table by the door. The two women would be in charge of collecting the money for the sale of these items and all proceeds from the auctions' winning bids.

"Martha."

She turned with surprise. "Annie! What are you doing here? You should be home resting!" Annie's time to have her baby was drawing near.

"I'm fine. You're my friend. I wanted to be here and help where I could." She grinned. "And to eat."

"Danki," Martha whispered, deeply touched that her friend had come.

The community women were kept busy selling craft items and food. The auctioneer was taking bids on pieces that Noah Lapp had donated from his furniture shop.

Day one passed quickly, and to Martha, it all seemed like a blur. Katie and Mae counted the proceeds. Thirty-two hundred dollars—a good start, they said. But would it be enough? Martha wondered as she lay in her bed later that night. The second day promised to be better, with the potential for higher profits.

On day two, her community held an Amish quilt auction, where the churchwomen donated food, quilts and other larger craft items they had made. English locals and tourists attended both events. Martha was more optimistic as she stood outside the gathering bidders and watched from the distance.

Quilts were hung on large wooden frames. She herself had donated one of her homemade quilts. She felt saddened to know that today someone would buy it. She'd had such hopes that someday she'd be able to use it in her child's room. It wasn't one made for a baby but a quilt large enough for a double bed that two children might have slept in.

Her quilt was on a display rack, like the others. Annie had told her yesterday that it had been Eli and Noah who'd made the racks.

The auctioneer for today's event was William Mast, a community member and Sarah Lapp's cousin. He spoke rapidly and confidently as he began his spiel. William described the item first, the type of quilt pattern and the name of the person who was responsible for its fine handiwork. Martha listened to William and was astonished at the way the crowd reacted favorably with bids, which started at four hundred dollars and continued to climb.

Martha fought tears as she watched. She'd thought life would be different, that Ike would be alive and that he would still love her...and they would have children—at least three. Instead, her husband had died and she was alone and determined to stay that way despite being in love with a man seven years her junior. He said that he loved her, but she couldn't believe it just because she wanted to.

"Martha."

She'd sensed Eli's presence before he'd spoken her name. She blinked rapidly to clear the remnants of her tears and turned to face him. "Those quilt racks you and Noah made..." She blushed as she met his gaze. "They're perfect."

He was silent as he studied her, his eyes narrowing as if he noticed that something had upset her and was debating what to do about it. The concern she felt emanating from him warmed her. She gave him a genuine smile.

"They weren't difficult to make, and we made them so they would come apart easily for next time." His features had softened. He glanced toward the auctioneer, who banged his gavel once, twice and a third time as he pronounced the quilt sold. "Wonderful," he murmured.

Martha hadn't heard the final price. "How much?"

"Nine hundred dollars."

She gasped. *"Ja?"* She grinned, feeling better about selling.

He smiled. "'Tis a beautiful quilt. We should do well today."

William announced the winning bid and again Martha's name as the craftswoman.

"That was yours," Eli said, looking impressed.

It didn't hurt so much now that she knew someone else treasured it enough to pay that much money for it. *"Ja,* I made it." She watched as two churchmen took her quilt down from the rack to give to the bid winner.

"Beautiful," he said softly.

She turned to him with a smile. *"Danki."* She felt sudden warmth at the look in his blue eyes. She had the strangest feeling that he'd referred to her and not the quilt.

Annie waved to her across the room. Martha nodded to Eli and left him for her friend. To her relief, he didn't follow. Emotion clogged her throat, and she didn't know how to deal with it.

The church elders and community women had deemed the two-day fundraising event successful. By five o'clock on the last day, everything brought to the auction had sold. The quilts had brought in the most money, but no one knew exactly how much yet.

Martha went home feeling hopeful. She would know more after Katie and Mae counted the money tomorrow. She climbed into bed that night with the belief that sleep would come easier to her. The last image in her mind was of Eli Lapp smiling and saying "beautiful."

Eli Lapp. What was she going to do about her feelings for Eli? *Nothing.* There was nothing she could do. Just because he'd implied that she was beautiful didn't change her doubts and fears regarding their relationship and her determination to remain alone.

The next morning, *Mam* and Mae King tallied up the money made at the two-day fundraiser. Eli hovered nearby, eager to know how well they did.

"Ninety-eight hundred dollars," Mae said. "It will be enough to make payments, but not enough to pay off the loan."

"What about the barn?" Eli asked as he approached.

Mae shook her head sadly. "We can take out what she'll need to rebuild her barn, but that will leave very little left to make her loan payments."

"I don't understand why Ike didn't tell her," *Mam* wondered aloud. "Didn't Martha get loan payment notices?"

"Nay," Mae said. "Apparently he had some special arrangement with the bank. He was to make a large payment after the spring planting, another one after the fall harvest. He had the money for the first payment, but then he died without telling his wife. Martha needed the funds to live and repair the house. She would have chosen differently if she'd known."

"Mae, you know that I don't speak ill of anyone, especially someone who has passed, but

I'm not feeling *gut* about what your brother-in-law did to Martha," Katie confessed, and Eli silently agreed.

Mae looked saddened. "Neither am I."

While the women shared a pot of tea and did one last tally recount, Eli wandered outside to mull over an idea that just occurred to him. His thoughts were in turmoil. He had saved more than twenty thousand dollars, which sat earning interest in a bank account. He could give Martha what she needed to rebuild her barn and pay off her loan. If he gave her the money, it would be years before he accumulated enough funds to start his carriage shop... And just at a time when he was close to finding a location.

He didn't struggle with indecision. He loved Martha, and he knew what he would do. He returned to the gathering room, where Mae and his mother were still discussing Martha's money.

"Mam?" he said when his mother looked up at his approach. "I have the money. I want to help Martha."

Mae widened her eyes. His mother, he saw, didn't appear surprised by his offer.

"How much?" *Mam* asked, her gaze filling with pride in her son.

"How much does she need?" He was prepared to give all if necessary.

"Fifteen thousand."

Eli nodded, unsurprised. He loved Martha, and she'd suffered enough in her life. He didn't want her to be burdened with worry. He would give her the money and gladly.

"We'll go to the bank together," he told his mother. "I'll withdraw the necessary funds, and then we'll get a cashier's check for People's Resident Bank." He kept his money in a different establishment. Helping Martha was important to him. His carriage shop could wait.

"I don't want her to know about any of this," Eli said. "She'll object, feel bad, and the last thing I want is for her to feel anything but relief." He saw his mother nod. "Mae?" He eyed their friend and neighbor, who was also Martha's sister-in-law.

"I won't say a word," Mae promised, her eyes welling with tears. "Except maybe to Amos and only if he asks, and I don't believe he will."

With that Eli had to be satisfied. "Shall we head to the bank?" Mae and his mother nodded. "Let's go then."

"It's a wonderful thing you're doing," Mae said.

He shrugged. To him, it was the most natural thing to want to give to the person he loved the most.

* * *

In the end, Mae and Katie asked Preacher Levi Stoltzfus to accompany them to present Martha with the check. Eli decided to tag along. He would hang back, because he didn't want her to suspect that he had anything to do with her good fortune.

The four of them—Katie, Mae, Levi and Eli—rode to Martha's farm, where they found Martha outside hanging laundry. Upon seeing their arrival, Martha dropped a garment into her laundry basket and approached.

"Hallo." Martha smiled at all of them. "Preacher Levi, what a nice surprise. I didn't expect to see you."

Levi smiled. "I've come to give the fundraiser money." He reached into the envelope given to Mae and Katie at the bank. "Here. I'm pleased to tell you that your bank loan has been paid, and there is enough left to build you a new barn."

Martha studied the check, her eyes widening with shock. "Truly?" she gasped. She was clearly amazed by the check amount. Eli knew that the sum was more than enough money for her barn. "And the bank loan is paid?" she whispered, her eyes filling.

The preacher nodded.

"Katie. Mae." Martha paused, blinking rapidly. "I—"

Eli understood her loss for words. He was pleased by her reaction. She would be fine, he thought, and he would be available to help. Martha wouldn't be any wiser that not all of the money had come from the fundraiser.

"Everyone helped," *Mam* reminded her.

Martha glanced in his direction. Eli smiled at her, and he saw something move across her expression. Then it was gone. *"Danki,"* she whispered, clearly overwhelmed. "I thought I'd be forced to sell the farm, but now I don't have to leave my home. Because of our Happiness community, my *haus* is safe and my animals will have a new place to live."

"We are pleased for you, Martha," Mae said.

"I don't know what to say."

"You don't have to say anything," Eli said. "We know you are thankful. It was the Lord who provided us with help. If it's all right with you, I'll have *Dat* stop in tomorrow to give you an estimate for your new barn."

Martha grinned. "That would be wonderful," she said, and her long look in his direction caused Eli's heart to beat rapidly with elation.

Seeing her smile, the joy in her brown eyes, gave him a rush of pleasure. He had made the right choice—the only choice for him. He would have to work hard to earn back what he'd given, but he didn't mind. Martha was worth everything.

* * *

Without the worry of the bank loan, Martha concentrated on her jelly business and preparing for the barn raising. She watched happily as several men in the community tore down the old stables. With help from Rick Martin and Jed's English construction boss, the churchmen were able to drag the charred metal farm equipment out of the ruined barn and into the pasture to be examined more closely.

"This one can be salvaged," Amos said. "'Tis black with soot, but it can be used as intended. We'll clean it up and you can keep it or sell it, Martha. 'Tis your choice."

She liked being given a choice, as if her opinion mattered. It hadn't with Ike, but these men were different. They were not trying to tell her what to do.

The other pieces of farm machinery were in poorer shape. "What about those?" Martha asked Matt Rhoades, Jedidiah's boss. Jed, Eli and Amos were eyeing the burned equipment.

"I'd suggest taking them to a recycling center," Matt said. "The center pays by weight. You should get a hefty amount."

Eli Lapp stood silently, watching Jed and Amos crouch low to study the charred metal. Martha found herself wanting to talk to him and ask his opinion on what she should do. She'd learned a lesson since the fire. A person shouldn't stand alone but should embrace what others have to offer. Just as she enjoyed helping out others, she had to learn that accepting help didn't make her weak.

It had been a while since she and Eli had spoken, and while she wished things were different between them, they weren't. Still, she had a right to seek a friend's advice anytime she wanted— didn't she? "What do you think?"

He appeared surprised that she'd asked his opinion. She'd been avoiding him lately, pretending that he wasn't close during church functions and other gatherings. She missed and loved him, and she realized she'd kept her distance because she was afraid that his interest in her was simply wishful thinking.

"I think you should consider what Matt said. You can use the money from the scrap metal to replace the damaged equipment with something serviceable and less fancy."

"Then that's what I'll do. *Danki*," she said with a smile of thanks. She was aware of his steady gaze on her as she returned to Matt. "I'd like to go with your suggestion. If you can arrange to take it to the recycling center, I'll pay your expenses and for your time."

Matt shook his head. "I want to help. There is no payment necessary."

Martha opened her mouth to object and then closed it. She would have to get past her determination to remain self-sufficient. No one could be entirely self-sufficient. Ike had tried to be when he'd shoveled that snow and died. "Thank you, Matt."

As she turned back, she saw Eli and Jedidiah head to the barn, where they proceeded to tug at the ruined siding. She couldn't tear her gaze away from Eli. She had seen a longing in his eyes as he'd studied her. She'd felt it, too—a longing for what couldn't be.

Samuel and his other sons conferred with Rick and Matt about the best transport for the scrap metal. Martha went inside the house and quickly poured drinks for the workers, who had to be thirsty after rummaging through the wreckage. She came out again with a tray of cups filled with iced tea.

"Is Eli going to buy that property for his shop?" Isaac asked Noah as they walked across the back lawn to the barn. She followed but kept her distance, still able to hear their conversation.

"*Nay*, he's decided to wait." Noah grabbed a hammer from his tool belt and used the claw end to pry nails from the siding. "Said he needs a few more years of work before he's satisfied with the money he's saved."

Martha halted in her tracks, unable to stop listening.

"But I thought you said he had enough money to go into business now." Isaac popped out a nail, and it fell to the ground.

"He says he's not in any hurry now," Noah said as he worked beside him. "Says he's content to work at my shop or for Matt with Jed. He'll find a better place in the next year or so."

Martha stood, frozen with tray in hand. *Eli had enough money to open his shop and now he doesn't?*

The news bothered her. And she began to think…about the fundraiser and the money made from the Amish auction. If she hadn't been so aware of Eli, she might not have noticed Eli's pleased expression when Preacher Levi had told her that they'd paid off her bank loan and presented her with the money for her barn.

Martha approached the men. "Iced tea!" she exclaimed loudly with a smile. She held out the tray. "I need to run an errand," she told them after they had accepted their drinks with murmured appreciation. "I shouldn't be gone long."

Samuel swallowed his mouthful of cold tea. "No rush. We have enough to keep us busy. I've ordered the lumber for the barn, and that cost is less than I figured. You should have enough money left to fix that lean-to in your back pasture."

Martha tried to look pleased. She had a suspicion that some of the money didn't come from the fundraiser, that someone—Eli—might have added funds of his own. "Sounds *gut*."

Her heart hammered hard as she climbed into her buggy and drove the distance to the Samuel Lapp farm. She stopped on the way to drop off some jelly and jam at Yoder's General Store before she continued on to have a talk with Katie Lapp, Eli's mother.

Katie was seated in a chair on the front porch shelling peas when Martha drove into the yard. "Afternoon, Katie," Martha greeted her.

"Martha! How nice to see you. How is the barn demolition going?"

"Fine. Most of the barn has been torn down. Jedidiah and Matt helped me to decide what to do with the ruined farm equipment." She climbed the porch and took the white rocker next to Katie's. She reached into the woman's pile of pea pods and began to shell peas.

She worked silently with the shelling for several minutes. "Katie?"

"There is something on your mind. What is it, Martha?"

Martha hesitated. "I have a question about the

fundraising money." She saw that Katie stopped what she was doing, looked at her.

"Ja?"

Did Martha imagine it or did Katie look mildly uncomfortable? Her suspicions intensified. "There wasn't enough money from the fundraiser," she said. "Was there? Someone added to the total to make sure I had what I needed."

Katie blinked. "Are you asking me?"

"Ja, I am." A fly flew near Martha's face, and she brushed it away. She studied Katie, waiting as the woman took her time before answering.

"'Tis true that there wasn't enough funds from the fundraisers." She opened a pea pod, slid her finger along the edge to loosen the peas and force them into a stainless steel bowl. "A few of us added a little." She grabbed another pea pod. "But one of us put in a large sum."

"Amos?" Martha asked, hoping that it was true.

Katie shook her head.

"Eli? Did your son use his shop money to help pay off my loan?"

The look on Katie's face gave her answer before she spoke. *"Ja."*

Martha was upset more than grateful. She swallowed hard. "How much? How much of his savings did he give away?"

"You should ask Eli."

"*Nay*, I want to know how much I need to pay him back."

But Katie was shaking her head. "He doesn't want to be paid back. He didn't want you to know, because he was afraid you'd refuse."

"And I would have," Martha admitted huskily as her throat tightened even more. "Why, Katie? Why would he sacrifice so much for me? Eli's young. He has his dream of opening a carriage shop. Why throw it away instead of opening his shop?"

Katie's expression grew soft. "Why do you think?"

Martha blinked as she continued to shell more peas. "I don't know why." The answer was there, but she didn't want to see it. "There are many young women within our community who think the world of Eli. He can have his pick of any one of them."

"And yet he hasn't shown an interest in them. But he has proven he cares for you."

Martha's face reddened. "I'm not the right woman for him."

Katie stopped and set the bowl on the small outdoor table beside her. "You don't like him?"

Martha felt her face and neck flush with fiery heat. "It's hard not to care about Eli." She loved him.

"Considering that my son gave away most of his hard-earned savings for you, I'd say he feels more than friendship for you." Katie stopped shelling peas to gaze at her steadily.

"I never encouraged him," Martha insisted.

"Martha," Katie began quietly. "Eli makes up his own mind. He's not asking for anything from you in return."

"I know." Martha blinked back tears as she leaned back in the rocking chair and closed her eyes. Immediately she envisioned Eli's expression as he told her that he cared for her, and she'd dismissed his feelings as if they weren't important to her. But they were important, almost too much. Her past relationships had made her wary, afraid. Neither John nor Ike would have sacrificed for her the way Eli had. If that wasn't proof of his love for her, what else could it be? Eli was a man, not a child. She didn't want to admit that.

"Do you have feelings for my *soohn*?" Katie asked.

Martha opened her eyes and met those of a concerned mother.

"*Ja.* I do. But I shouldn't. I'm a widow who is too old for him. He deserves better than a woman who can't give him what he needs."

Katie raised her eyebrows. "You are what— five or six years older?"

"Seven."

The woman smiled. "Hardly a huge difference. You married a man who was your senior by more than ten years, *ja*?" Her expression and tone softened. "It's been months since Ike died. No one would be upset if you chose to marry again. After their wives pass on, the men in our community often choose to wed again quickly, sometimes for the sake of the children but more often than not, I think, because they miss having a life partner."

"The age difference between Ike and me is different than between Eli and me."

Her friend looked curious. "How?"

"Eli is not an old spinster who was grateful to be any man's wife."

A lengthy silence ensued.

"You love him." Katie eyed her with satisfaction.

Martha stood, went to the porch railing to gaze out over the yard. "Does it matter if I do?"

"If you love my *soohn*, *ja*, it matters."

Martha spun to face her. "Why?"

"Because Eli loves you. If you have any doubts at all, know this—he wouldn't have given fifteen thousand dollars of his money to just anyone. *Nay*, he gave it to you because he loves you. He didn't want you to know. It wasn't a bid for your affection but a genuine act of selflessness and love. Mae and I are the only ones who know."

Katie rubbed the back of her neck. "And now you. The last person he wanted to know."

"Fifteen thousand dollars?" Martha gasped. It took her several seconds to process that the man she loved had given away that much money... for her. If his gift wasn't a true testament of his love, then what else could it be?

Katie looked suddenly uncomfortable. "I shouldn't have told you. He'll be upset with me." She firmed her lips. "But you asked and I'll not lie."

"He loves me that much?" Now that her suspicions were founded, Martha knew she had to do something.

"Ja, he does."

"Danki." Martha had a plan to give Eli back his money.

Eli's mother looked concerned. "What are you going to do?"

Martha smiled in reassurance. "Nothing to hurt the man I love."

She left then, her mind wildly active with what she had to do. It was too late to cancel the barn raising. *But it's not too late to sell the farm.*

Chapter Nineteen

~∙~

Eli eyed Martha's new barn with satisfaction. The building was larger than before and better constructed. The men of his community had begun work early that morning and continued until it was done.

The women fed the workers on and off all day. Martha, he saw, kept busy scurrying to keep food on the table. Eli had kept his distance from her. He hadn't eaten when she was serving. He'd eaten when one of his cousins had worked the food table, and then he'd hurried back to work before Martha could catch sight of him.

He was pleased to help with the barn raising, glad that Martha had no idea of his part in making sure she had enough money. It had been a long day but a productive one. He transferred his gaze from the new building to the women gathering up the empty dishes. This would be his last day he'd get to see Martha on a daily basis. With that knowledge hovering in his mind, Eli gave in to the urge to talk with her.

Martha stood in the barnyard, thanking Amos and his family for their hard work.

"It took many skilled hands to craft this barn in one day," Amos said, brushing off his part in the day's labor.

Eli hung back as Martha said goodbye to the other workers and their families. Soon the only ones left were his family. She turned only to stop short when she saw him standing within a few feet of her.

"Martha," he said.

"Eli!" she gasped as if taken by surprise. "I didn't know you were behind me." Her look made him squirm as if he'd done something wrong by keeping silent behind her. "You worked hard today," she said with a sudden smile. *"Danki."*

He shrugged. "No harder than the rest."

"I don't have to worry about leaks now," Martha said softly, and he was instantly reminded of the storm and their time in the barn together. Something thick and tense rose in the air between them.

Feelings intensified in Eli, overwhelming him with the love she didn't want. He stepped back, putting distance between them. "I'm glad everything turned out well for you."

She nodded. "I'm sincerely grateful for my *gut* fortune."

"Eli! Are you ready?" His father stood by the family wagon with his mother in the passenger seat; his younger brothers and sister sat in the back with the tools.

"Coming, *Dat*!" He hesitated, unwilling to leave her. If only things were different and she'd give him half a chance. "I have to go." When she didn't answer, he forced a smile, then headed toward their vehicle, where he climbed into the back with his siblings. His father stepped up into the front and took up the reins.

Eli stared at Martha, wondering at the odd look he saw on her face as he turned. Would she miss him? Except for church and visiting Sundays, there'd be little chance for them to see each other or spend any time together.

As his father drove away from the farm, Eli stared out the back of the wagon until Martha was but a speck in his line of vision as the vehicle turned down the road toward home.

Martha still cared too deeply for her late husband to consider another man in her life. He would honor her wishes and leave her alone. He would work hard to save for Lapp's

Buggy Shop. He only hoped that someday he would be able to get over her.

The day after the barn raising, Martha spoke with a Realtor about selling the farm. She couldn't live there now that she knew it was Eli's hard-earned carriage shop money that had made it possible for her to stay. So she would sell the property, pay Eli back his money and find another place to live. She could stay for a time with her in-laws. She could return home to Indiana and face her sister and her sister's husband or she could remain in Happiness and find a much smaller home.

The idea of living in a bungalow appealed to Martha. She'd always thought Ike's house too big and too cold. She'd find and move into a cottage. She'd continue to make and sell jellies without the added worry of managing a farm.

She had to pay back Eli. She wouldn't rest until she sold the farm and returned his money. She knew that the Lord approved of her plan when she received an offer for the property within two days of its listing. The original owner's children wanted to buy back the house and land. Now that their father had passed on, the property held sentimental value for them, as their father had built the home for their mother, who had died before it was finished. Devastated by the loss, the man had stopped all construction and put the unfinished house up for sale. Ike, who'd wanted to move back to Happiness after his first wife's death, had been the one who had purchased the property. And then Ike had married her, and the house had become their home.

For the next few weeks, Eli built hog houses for Matt Rhoades's construction company. The money was decent, and the work was consistent. He took every hour he could get and deposited the majority of his pay into his bank account. He was determined to open his carriage shop. It wouldn't be tomorrow or the day after, but eventually he would have his shop.

"Eli." Jedidiah came around from the other side of the block foundation they'd constructed for the pole building. "Are you ready to go home?"

"*Ja*. 'Tis been a long day, but we got a lot done."

"*Ja*, Matt is pleased. He says you're a *gut* worker."

"'Tis a way to earn money."

His brother narrowed his gaze. "What happened to your shop?"

"I still plan to open it. Why?"

"Well, to hear Noah tell it, you were all fired

up about a place you'd found and then suddenly you changed your mind."

"I haven't changed my mind. I want to earn a little extra cash first—that's all."

Jedidiah nodded in understanding as they headed with tools in hand to Jedidiah's market wagon. Eli was glad that Jed had driven today. The other family vehicles were in use, except for the two-wheeled courting buggy that needed work, which Eli planned to start on first thing in the morning.

"We've got a few days before Matt wants to start the next job," Jed said as Eli climbed down from the buggy in their parents' yard. "Are you in? Or will you be working at Noah's?"

"I'm in if Noah doesn't need me."

Jedidiah frowned. "What's with you? You haven't been yourself lately."

"I'm fine."

"*Nay, bruder.* You're not." He studied Eli through narrowed eyes. "Must be a girl." He smiled. "Martha King. You're sweet on her."

"Go home," Eli said grumpily. He turned and was startled to see Martha exit his parents' house and head in his direction.

"Afternoon, Martha," Jed said pleasantly.

"*Hallo*, Jed." She gave him a nod, then turned. "Eli."

"I'm surprised to see you," Eli said. It had

been weeks since they'd last spoken. He'd seen her from a distance at church and visiting Sundays, but he wasn't about to pursue someone who didn't want to be chased.

"I've got to get home. See you at Noah's tomorrow, Eli," Jed said. He nodded. "Martha."

Eli said goodbye to his eldest brother, then turned to eye Martha warily. "Why are you here?" He saw her frown and a hurt look enter her brown eyes. "I'm sorry. That didn't come out right. May I start again? 'Tis nice to see you, Martha. I haven't spoken with you in ages."

She seemed suddenly nervous. "I'm here to see you."

"You are?" Eli stared at her. He could never get his fill of looking at her, spending time in her company.

"Why haven't you opened your carriage shop yet?" she burst out, startling him.

"I—ah—will. I'm still working to save money."

She looked pretty in her green dress, white head covering and white cape with white apron. She didn't comment on his need to work and save.

"How's the barn?" he asked, not knowing what else to say.

"Barn's still standing. I hear the rain didn't touch the inside the other day."

He frowned. "You hear?"

Martha nodded. "Not my barn anymore. I'm staying with Amos and Mae until I'm ready to move into my own place. I sold the farm."

"You what?" Eli was flabbergasted. She'd sold the farm! "You're going to move away."

She gazed at him, her brown eyes intent, a strange little smile on her lips. "I stopped by because I have something to give you."

He gazed his fill of her and yearned for more. "You're going home to Indiana?"

"Would you miss me if I did?" she teased.

"*Ja*, I would," he admitted, feeling all his love for her inside.

"Eli—"

"Martha, I don't want you to go."

She regarded him with affection. "Eli, did I say I was going anywhere?"

He stared at her, confused.

"Here." She shoved an envelope into his hand.

He accepted the envelope, careful to avoid touching her. "What is it?" He'd been working all day, and he felt grimy and sweaty. He wished she'd come after he'd showered and changed. But she was here now, and he was grateful that for whatever reason she'd sought him out.

"Open it, Eli," she urged when he made no move to do so.

He reluctantly looked away from her pretty

face to study the envelope. Slowly, he ran a finger along the sealed edge, lifting it to display a piece of paper inside. He frowned.

"Take it out," Martha ordered. *"Please."*

He obeyed, extracting the document carefully. He recognized a bank check and met her gaze with widened eyes.

"What's this for?" It was a lot of money—twenty-five thousand dollars, in fact.

"It's the money I owe you with interest."

"Martha—"

"Eli, you sacrificed your shop savings to help me. 'Twas the sweetest and most thoughtful thing that anyone has ever done for me."

"But the money—"

"'Tis from the sale of the farm." She raised a hand to stop him from talking. "I never wanted that big place, Eli. That was my late husband's home. I never felt like I belonged there. I much prefer a smaller *haus* like Jacob and Annie's or Noah and Rachel's. I couldn't continue to live in a place I didn't like after learning what you'd done for me."

"I don't know what to say."

"You don't have to say a thing. When I figured out that you were the one responsible for paying off the loan and rebuilding my barn, I felt…" She blinked back tears. *"Cherished,"* she whispered, her eyes glistening.

He experienced a warm sensation. "You are cherished, Martha."

"I know," she said. "By you."

He nodded as hope filled his heart. "I love you, Martha."

"I know," she said. "You couldn't have convinced me any better. I realized that love is more important than age difference, and that love means taking a risk, and I'm willing to take it now. I'm willing to risk it all…for you." She blinked up at him, her expression earnest. "I love you, Eli."

"Then you'll be staying," he said with a grin. She nodded. "And letting me court you?"

"Only if you willingly take the money and more if I want to give it. Open your carriage shop, Eli. Do what you've always wanted to do."

"It just doesn't seem ri—"

She placed two fingers over his mouth to silence him. "If you love me, then you'll take this money and talk with Noah. He has a better idea of where to set up your shop."

"You talked with Noah?"

Martha nodded. "And your *mam* and *dat*…and Jacob, Isaac, Daniel, Joseph and Hannah—and Jedidiah. I talked with him, too, the other day."

Eli stared. "Why?"

She shrugged. "Because I wanted to get to know better the family of the man I love."

He grinned. "'Cause you're going to be part of my family."

Martha raised her eyebrows, but he saw the joy in her face. "Am I?"

"Ja," he said huskily, drawing her into his arms. "If I have anything to say or do about it, you will be the most important part." He smiled against her hair as she leaned her head against his check. "Don't think because you're older that you'll be heading our household."

She lifted her head, her brown eyes twinkling. "I wouldn't think of it."

His lips twitched. "We'll see." And then he kissed her to show her who was boss.

Epilogue

Happiness, Pennsylvania
Eleven months later

Eli Lapp examined the pony cart with a critical eye. Abram Peachy's daughter Rose Ann had driven the carriage into a ditch along the front side of her father's property. Fortunately for Rosie—and Abram—neither the child nor the horse was hurt. However, the same couldn't be said for the cart's front right wheel.

He pulled out his measuring tape to gauge the wheel size. He took note of the measurement with satisfaction. He had the right size in stock. He would change the wheel and check over every inch of the vehicle to make sure everything was fixed and safe. Lapp's Buggy Shop had been open for business for almost a year now, and he would never rush a job and risk a customer's safety. Serving his community gave Eli a deep sense of satisfaction, as did his marriage to Martha. He smiled as he thought of his wife, which he did nearly every second of every day. She was the constant joy in his life, and he was pleased to know that she was as happy in their marriage as he was.

A quick glance at the wall clock in his work area confirmed that it was lunchtime. He smiled. He could change the wheel and walk home to enjoy his wife's delicious cooking before finishing his workday. Eli stuck a wooden wedge under the bent wheel, raising it off the ground. Then, using tools of his trade, he removed it, set it aside and went to find the correct replacement, which he slipped on and fastened properly. Satisfied with the work, he washed his face and hands in the sink. He locked the front door, hung the out-to-lunch sign, then exited by the back, locked up and headed toward home.

Home was the three-bedroom cottage a short distance from the shop. He paused a moment to gaze happily at Noah's furniture business next door. It had been Noah's idea to build Eli's business close to his, and it had been a good one. Living near each other, Martha and Rachel had become fast friends. He saw no sign of Noah or Rachel, so he strode the rest of the way to the house his family had built for Martha and him. It was comfortable, cozy and just what they needed. White siding with no shutters, it wasn't a house; it was their home.

"Martha?" he called as he entered through their back door.

To Eli's delight, she came from the direction of their gathering room, her eyes lighting up with pleasure when she saw him.

"You're home!" She glided close, a lovely vision of impending motherhood. It was the early stages of her pregnancy, but he could see her small belly bump, see the joy of carrying their child that radiated from her pretty features. During their courtship, she'd confided about her fear that she couldn't conceive and how she'd blamed herself for not giving Ike a son. With the Lord's help, he'd been able to convince her that, child or not, he would love her for always.

Eli met her halfway and opened his arms, and she slid into his embrace as if she'd been longing for it. As he pressed his face against her forehead, he inhaled her fragrance, her homemade soap scented with a hint of chocolate and the ever-present smell he loved the most—the sweet scent of her. He could feel her heart beating wildly. He heard the soft exhalation and inhalation of her breath, and he silently offered to the Lord another prayer of thanks. He continued to thank Him every day.

Martha pulled away from his arms and he immediately let her go. "You're home early."

He smiled. "*Nay*, love. I'm late." He wondered what she'd been doing. "Working on the quilt for our baby?"

"*Ja*, it will take me until she's born to finish it."

He raised his eyebrow. "She?"

She grinned. "Or he? It doesn't matter as long as our child is healthy."

"Amen," he murmured.

He reached for her hand, pulled her gently toward the door. "Come with me," he urged.

"Where?" she asked as she trustingly followed his lead.

"To the shop."

She frowned. "Didn't *ya* just come from there?"

"*Ja*, love, but there is something new I want to show you."

She gazed at him affectionately as he led her the short distance. He smiled at her obvious curiosity.

"Bob Whittier said there have been youngsters breaking into shops," he said as he unlocked the back entrance. "Could be just a prank, but I don't want to take chances."

Gazing at her husband, Martha placed a hand against her belly, the fluttery feeling she was having had nothing to do with their unborn child. Eli always affected her like that. She'd never realized that married life could be this good. She'd had a calm and safe, if declining, marriage with Ike, but with Eli, her husband's attention thrilled her like nothing else on this earth.

"Close your eyes," he whispered into her ear.

She obeyed and felt a tingling from the nape of her neck downward.

"Careful now as we go inside," he warned softly, lovingly, as he steered her carefully through the open door. "We're heading to the side room."

"May I open my eyes yet?" Excitement pulsed through her veins, heightening her awareness of him. Eli was always doing special things for her.

The room was the smallest in the building; she'd been inside many times since the shop was built. Eli stopped her and released her hand to place his arm around her shoulders. "There," he said with satisfaction. "Open your eyes."

She did. "Oh my." Two wooden chests, one large enough to hold an adult's clothing, the other the same style but much smaller as one might have for a child…or a baby, stood before her.

"Oh, Eli…" Her eyes filled with tears. "You made these for us. How did you find the time?"

"Noah's shop is across the parking lot. I'd slip over for an hour or two each day to work on them." She met his gaze, saw him studying her with intensely bright blue eyes. "You like them?"

"I love them." She sniffed, and tears trickled down her checks.

He frowned. "Then why are you crying?"

"These are happy tears, husband."

His whole body seemed to sigh with relief. Following him outside, Martha waited while he locked the building before reaching for her hand. They headed toward their cottage. Eli stopped suddenly, tugged on her hand to stop her. "Look," he said, pointing.

She followed the direction of his gaze and smiled. A family of red foxes with baby cubs played in the grass along the edge of their property. "They're beautiful," she whispered, understanding his excitement.

"They're a family, like we are," Eli said. He slipped his arm about her waist and drew her closer. "We are truly blessed."

Martha felt small, delicate and truly loved. *"Ja."*

"I love you, Martha."

"I know." She grinned at him, and he returned his attention to the fox family. She enjoyed the companionable silence between them, felt her love for Eli down to her soul. "I love you, Eli."

His handsome features lit up like a child's who'd been offered his favorite treat. "Thanks be to *Gott*."

Then together they crossed the yard, entered their humble home and went on to enjoy a life of laughter and love by the grace of the good Lord.

* * * * *

Dear Reader,

The Amish village of Happiness, Pennsylvania, is one of my favorite places. I'm fortunate that every time I write, I enjoy a visit with the Samuel Lapp family and other members of their Old Order Amish community. In my last Lancaster County Wedding series book, I told Jacob Lapp's story and about his efforts to win Annie Zook, the girl he's loved since he was a young boy. This book belongs to Elijah, Jacob's fraternal twin. Elijah isn't interested in love at this stage in his life, and he certainly doesn't expect to find it in Martha, Ike King's widow. But God has other plans for him, just as He had for his brothers, Jedidiah, Noah and Jacob.

I hope you enjoy Eli's story as much as I loved writing it. And if you haven't done so already, you can visit Happiness again by reading *Noah's Sweetheart*, *Jedidiah's Bride* and *A Wife for Jacob*.

I wish you joy and all of the good that life has to offer. May God hold and keep you in the palm of His hand.

Blessings and light,
Rebecca Kertz

LARGER-PRINT BOOKS!

GET 2 FREE LARGER-PRINT NOVELS PLUS 2 FREE MYSTERY GIFTS

Love Inspired®

SUSPENSE
RIVETING INSPIRATIONAL ROMANCE

Larger-print novels are now available...

REQUEST YOUR FREE BOOKS!
2 FREE WHOLESOME ROMANCE NOVELS
IN LARGER PRINT
PLUS 2
FREE
MYSTERY GIFTS

⁂⁂⁂⁂⁂⁂⁂⁂⁂⁂⁂⁂⁂⁂⁂⁂⁂⁂⁂⁂⁂

HEARTWARMING™
⁂⁂⁂⁂⁂⁂⁂⁂⁂⁂⁂⁂⁂⁂⁂⁂⁂⁂⁂⁂⁂

Wholesome, tender romances

YES! Please send me 2 FREE Harlequin® Heartwarming Larger-Print novels and my 2 FREE mystery gifts (gifts worth about $10). After receiving them, if I don't wish to receive any more books, I can return the shipping statement marked "cancel." If I don't cancel, I will receive 4 brand-new larger-print novels every month and be billed just $5.24 per book in the U.S. or $5.99 per book in Canada. That's a savings of at least 19% off the cover price. It's quite a bargain! Shipping and handling is just 50¢ per book in the U.S. and 75¢ per book in Canada.* I understand that accepting the 2 free books and gifts places me under no obligation to buy anything. I can always return a shipment and cancel at any time. Even if I never buy another book, the two free books and gifts are mine to keep forever.

161/361 IDN GHX2

Name _____ (PLEASE PRINT) _____

Address _____ Apt. # _____

City _____ State/Prov. _____ Zip/Postal Code _____

Signature (if under 18, a parent or guardian must sign) _____

Mail to the **Reader Service:**
IN U.S.A.: P.O. Box 1867, Buffalo, NY 14240-1867
IN CANADA: P.O. Box 609, Fort Erie, Ontario L2A 5X3

* Terms and prices subject to change without notice. Prices do not include applicable taxes. Sales tax applicable in N.Y. Canadian residents will be charged applicable taxes. Offer not valid in Quebec. This offer is limited to one order per household. Not valid for current subscribers to Harlequin Heartwarming larger-print books. All orders subject to credit approval. Credit or debit balances in a customer's account(s) may be offset by any other outstanding balance owed by or to the customer. Please allow 4 to 6 weeks for delivery. Offer available while quantities last.

Your Privacy—The Reader Service is committed to protecting your privacy. Our Privacy Policy is available online at www.ReaderService.com or upon request from the Reader Service.

We make a portion of our mailing list available to reputable third parties that offer products we believe may interest you. If you prefer that we not exchange your name with third parties, or if you wish to clarify or modify your communication preferences, please visit us at www.ReaderService.com/consumerchoice or write to us at Reader Service Preference Service, P.O. Box 9062, Buffalo, NY 14240-9062. Include your complete name and address.

YES! Please send me **The Montana Mavericks Collection** in Larger Print. This collection begins with 3 FREE books and 2 FREE gifts (gifts valued at approx. $20.00 retail) in the first shipment, along with the other first 4 books from the collection! If I do not cancel, I will receive 8 monthly shipments until I have the entire 51-book Montana Mavericks collection. I will receive 2 or 3 FREE books in each shipment and I will pay just $4.99 US/ $5.89 CDN for each of the other four books in each shipment, plus $2.99 for shipping and handling per shipment.*If I decide to keep the entire collection, I'll have paid for only 32 books, because 19 books are FREE! I understand that accepting the 3 free books and gifts places me under no obligation to buy anything. I can always return a shipment and cancel at any time. My free books and gifts are mine to keep no matter what I decide.

263 HCN 2404   463 HCN 2404

Name	(PLEASE PRINT)	
Address		Apt. #
City	State/Prov.	Zip/Postal Code

Signature (if under 18, a parent or guardian must sign)

Mail to the **Reader Service**:

IN U.S.A.: P.O. Box 1867, Buffalo, NY 14240-1867
IN CANADA: P.O. Box 609, Fort Erie, Ontario L2A 5X3

READERSERVICE.COM

Manage your account online!

- Review your order history
- Manage your payments
- Update your address

*We've designed the
Reader Service website
just for you.*

Enjoy all the features!

- Discover new series available to you, and read excerpts from any series.
- Respond to mailings and special monthly offers.
- Connect with favorite authors at the blog.
- Browse the Bonus Bucks catalog and online-only exculsives.
- Share your feedback.

Visit us at:
ReaderService.com

RS15